ELLEN G. WHITE

THE GREAT CONTROVERSY

ELLEN G. WHITE

THE GREAT CONTROVERSY

THE GREAT CONTROVERSY

By

ELLEN G. WHITE

Contents

"The Great Controversy

Between

Christ and His Angels,

and

Satan and His Angels."

CHAPTER 1

The Fall of Satan

The Lord has shown me that Satan was once an honored angel in heaven, next to Jesus Christ. His countenance was mild, expressive of happiness like the other angels. His forehead was high and broad, and showed great intelligence. His form was perfect. He had noble, majestic bearing. And I saw that when God said to his Son, Let us make man in our image, Satan was jealous of Jesus. He wished to be consulted concerning the formation of man. He was filled with envy, jealousy and hatred. He wished to be the highest in heaven, next to God, and receive the highest honors. Until this time all heaven was in order, harmony and perfect subjection to the government of God.

It was the highest sin to rebel against the order and will of God. All heaven seemed in commotion. The angels were marshaled in companies with a commanding angel at their head. All the angels were astir. Satan was insinuating against the government of God, ambitious to exalt himself, and unwilling to submit to the authority of Jesus. Some of the angels sympathized with Satan in his rebellion, and others strongly contended for the honor and wisdom of God in giving authority to his Son. And there was contention with the angels. Satan and his affected ones, who were striving to reform the government of God, wished to look into his unsearchable wisdom to ascertain his purpose in exalting Jesus, and endowing him with such unlimited power and command. They rebelled against the authority of the Son of God, and all the angels were summoned to appear before the Father, to have their cases decided. And it was decided that Satan should be expelled from heaven, and that the angels, all who joined with Satan in the rebellion, should be turned out with him. Then there was war in heaven. Angels were engaged in the battle; Satan wished to conquer the Son of God, and those who were submissive to his will. But the good and true angels prevailed, and Satan, with his followers, was driven from heaven.

After Satan was shut out of heaven, with those who fell with him, he realized that he had lost all the purity and glory of heaven forever. Then he repented and wished to be

1

reinstated again in heaven. He was willing to take his proper place, or any place that might be assigned him. But no, heaven must not be placed in jeopardy. All heaven might be marred should he be taken back; for sin originated with him, and the seeds of rebellion were within him. Satan had obtained followers, those who sympathized with him in his rebellion. He and his followers repented, wept and implored to be taken back into the favor of God. But no, their sin, their hate, their envy and jealousy, had been so great that God could not blot it out. It must remain to receive its final punishment.

When Satan became fully conscious that there was no possibility of his being brought again into favor with God, then his malice and hatred began to be manifest. He consulted with his angels, and a plan was laid to still work against God's government. When Adam and Eve were placed in the beautiful garden, Satan was laying plans to destroy them. A consultation was held with his evil angels. In no way could this happy couple be deprived of their happiness if they obeyed God. Satan could not exercise his power upon them unless they should first disobey God, and forfeit his favor. They must devise some plan to lead them to disobedience that they might incur God's frown and be brought under the more direct influence of Satan and his angels. It was decided that Satan should assume another form, and manifest an interest for man. He must insinuate against God's truthfulness, create doubt whether God did mean as he said, next, excite their curiosity, and lead them to pry into the unsearchable plans of God, which Satan had been guilty of, and reason as to the cause of his restrictions in regard to the tree of knowledge.

See Isaiah 14:12-20; Ezekiel 28:1-19; Revelation 12:7-9

CHAPTER 2

The Fall of Man

I saw that the holy angels often visited the garden, and gave instruction to Adam and Eve concerning their employment, and also taught them concerning the rebellion of Satan and his fall. The angels warned them of Satan, and cautioned them not to separate from each other in their employment, for they might be brought in contact with this fallen foe. The angels enjoined upon them to closely follow the directions God had given them, for in perfect obedience only were they safe. And if they were obedient, this fallen foe could have no power over them.

Satan commenced his work with Eve, to cause her to disobey. She first erred in wandering from her husband, next, in lingering around the forbidden tree, and next in listening to the voice of the tempter, and even daring to doubt what God had said - In the day that thou eatest thereof thou shalt surely die. She thought, Perhaps it does not mean just as the Lord said. She ventured to disobey. She put forth her hand, took of the fruit, and ate. It was pleasing to the eye, and pleasant to the taste. She was jealous that God had withheld from them what was really for their good. She offered the fruit to her husband, thereby tempting him. She related to Adam all that the serpent had said, and expressed her astonishment that he had the power of speech.

I saw a sadness came over Adam's countenance. He appeared afraid and astonished. A struggle appeared to be going on in his mind. He felt sure that this was the foe which they had been warned against, and that his wife must die. They must be separated. His love for Eve was strong. And in utter discouragement he resolved to share her fate. He seized the fruit, and quickly ate it. Then Satan exulted. He had rebelled in heaven, and had sympathizers who loved him, and followed him in his rebellion. He fell, and caused others to fall with him. And he had now tempted the woman to distrust God, to inquire into his wisdom, and to seek to penetrate his all-wise plans. Satan knew the woman would not fall alone. Adam, through his love for Eve, disobeyed the command of God and fell with her.

The news of man's fall spread through heaven. Every harp was hushed. The angels cast their crowns from their heads in sorrow. All heaven was in agitation. A counsel was held to decide what must be done with the guilty pair. The angels feared that they would put forth the hand, and eat of the tree of life, and be immortal sinners. But God said that he would drive the transgressors from the garden. Angels were commissioned immediately to guard the way of the tree of life. It had been Satan's studied plan that Adam and Eve should disobey God, receive his frown, and then be led on to partake of the tree of life, that they might live forever in sin and disobedience, and thus sin be immortalized. But holy angels were sent to drive them out of the garden, while another company of angels were commissioned to guard the way to the tree of life. Each of these mighty angels appeared to have something in their right hand, which looked like a glittering sword.

Then Satan triumphed. Others he had made to suffer by his fall. He had been shut out of heaven, they out of Paradise.

See Genesis chap.3

CHAPTER 3

The Plan of Salvation

Sorrow filled heaven, as it was realized that man was lost, and the world that God created was to be filled with mortals doomed to misery, sickness and death, and there was no way of escape for the offender. The whole family of Adam must die. I saw the lovely Jesus, and beheld an expression of sympathy and sorrow upon his countenance. Soon I saw him approach the exceeding bright light which enshrouded the Father. Said my accompanying angel, He is in close converse with His Father. The anxiety of the angels seemed to be intense while Jesus was communing with his Father. Three times he was shut in by the glorious light about the Father, and the third time he came from the Father, his person could be seen. His countenance was calm, free from all perplexity and trouble, and shone with benevolence and loveliness, such as words cannot express. He then made known to the angelic host that a way of escape had been made for lost man. He told them that he had been pleading with his Father, and had offered to give his life a ransom, and take the sentence of death upon himself, that through him man might find pardon. That through the merits of his blood, and obedience to the law of God, they could have the favor of God, and be brought into the beautiful garden, and eat of the fruit of the tree of life.

At first the angels could not rejoice, for their commander concealed nothing from them, but opened before them the plan of salvation. Jesus told them that he would stand between the wrath of his Father and guilty man, that he would bear iniquity and scorn, and but few would receive him as the Son of God. Nearly all would hate and reject him. He would leave all his glory in heaven, appear upon earth as a man, humble himself as a man, become acquainted by His own experience with the various temptations with which man would be beset, that he might know how to succor those who should be tempted; and that finally, after his mission as a teacher should be accomplished, he would be delivered into the hands of men, and endure almost every cruelty and suffering that Satan and his angels could inspire wicked men to inflict; that he should die the cruelest of deaths, hung up between the heavens and the earth as a guilty sinner; that he should suffer dreadful hours of agony, which even angels could not look upon, but would vail their faces from the sight. Not merely agony of body would he suffer; but mental agony, that with which bodily suffering could in no wise be compared. The weight of the sins of the whole world would be upon him. He told them he would die and rise again the third day, and should ascend to his Father to intercede for wayward, guilty man.

The angels prostrated themselves before him. They offered their lives. Jesus said to them that he should by his death save many; that the life of an angel could not pay the debt. His life alone could be accepted of his Father as a ransom for man.

Jesus also told them that they should have a part to act, to be with him, and at different times strengthen him. That he should take man's fallen nature, and his strength would not be even equal with theirs. And they should be witnesses of his humiliation and great sufferings. And as they should witness his sufferings, and the hate of men towards him, they would be stirred with the deepest emotions, and through their love for him, would wish to rescue, and deliver him from his murderers; but that they must not interfere to prevent anything they should behold; and that they should act a part in his resurrection; that the plan of salvation was devised, and his Father had accepted the plan.

With a holy sadness, Jesus comforted and cheered the angels, and informed them that hereafter those whom he should redeem would be with him, and ever dwell with him; and that by his death he should ransom many, and destroy him who had the power of death. And his Father would give him the kingdom, and the greatness of the kingdom under the whole heaven, and he should possess it forever and ever. Satan and sinners should be destroyed, never more to disturb heaven, or the purified, new earth. Jesus bid the heavenly host be reconciled to the plan that his Father accepted, and rejoice that fallen man could be exalted again through his death, to obtain favor with God and enjoy heaven.

Then joy, inexpressible joy, filled heaven. And the heavenly host sung a song of praise and adoration. They touched their harps and sung a note higher than they had done before, for the great mercy and condescension of God in yielding up his dearly Beloved to die for a race of rebels. Praise and adoration were poured forth for the self-denial and sacrifice of Jesus; that he would consent to leave the bosom of his Father, and choose a life of suffering and anguish, and die an ignominious death to give life to others.

Said the angel, Think ye that the Father yielded up his dearly beloved Son without a struggle? No, no. It was even a struggle with the God of heaven, whether to let guilty man perish, or to give his beloved Son to die for them. Angels were so interested for man's salvation that there could be found among them those who would yield their glory, and give their life for perishing man. But, said my accompanying angel, that would avail nothing. The transgression was so great that an angel's life would not pay the debt. Nothing but the death and intercessions of his Son would pay the debt, and save lost man from hopeless sorrow and misery.

But the work of the angels was assigned them, to ascend and descend with strengthening balm from glory to soothe the Son of God in his sufferings, and administer unto him. Also, their work would be to guard and keep the subjects of grace from the evil angels, and the darkness constantly thrown around them by Satan. I saw that it was impossible for God to alter or change his law, to save lost, perishing man; therefore he suffered his beloved Son to die for man's transgression.

Satan again rejoiced with his angels that he could, by causing man's fall, pull down the Son of God from his exalted position. He told his angels that when Jesus should take fallen man's nature, he could overpower him, and hinder the accomplishment of the plan of salvation.

I was then shown Satan as he was, a happy, exalted angel. Then I was shown him as he now is. He still bears a kingly form. His features are still noble, for he is an angel fallen. But the expression of his countenance is full of anxiety, care, unhappiness, malice, hate, mischief, deceit, and every evil. That brow which was once so noble, I particularly noticed. His forehead commenced from his eyes to recede backward. I saw that he had demeaned himself so long, that every good quality was debased, and every evil trait was developed. His eyes were cunning, sly, and showed great penetration. His frame was large, but the flesh hung loosely about his hands and face. As I beheld him, his chin was resting upon his left hand. He appeared to be in deep thought. A smile was upon his countenance, which made me tremble, it was so full of evil, and Satanic slyness. This smile is the one he wears just before he makes sure of his victim, and as he fastens the victim in his snare, this smile grows horrible.

See Isaiah chap.53

CHAPTER 4

The First Advent of Christ

Then I was carried down to the time when Jesus was to take upon himself man's nature, humble himself as a man, and suffer the temptations of Satan.

His birth was without worldly grandeur. He was born in a stable, cradled in a manger; yet his birth was honored far above any of the sons of men. Angels from heaven informed the shepherds of the advent of Jesus, while the light and glory from God accompanied their testimony. The heavenly host touched their harps and glorified God. They triumphantly heralded the advent of the Son of God to a fallen world to accomplish the work of redemption, and by his death bring peace, happiness, and everlasting life to man. God honored the advent of his Son. Angels worshiped him.

Angels of God hovered over the scene of his baptism, and the Holy Spirit descended in the shape of a dove, and lighted upon him, and as the people stood greatly amazed, with their eyes fastened upon him, the Father's voice was heard from heaven, saying, Thou art my beloved Son, in thee I am well pleased.

John was not certain that it was the Saviour who came to be baptized of him in Jordan. But God had promised him a sign by which he should know the Lamb of God. That sign was given as the heavenly Dove rested upon Jesus, and the glory of God shone round about him. John reached forth his hand, pointing to Jesus, and with a loud voice cried out, Behold the Lamb of God which taketh away the sin of the world.

John informed his disciples that Jesus was the promised Messiah, the Saviour of the world. As his work was closing, he taught his disciples to look to Jesus, and follow him as the great teacher. John's life was without pleasure. It was sorrowful and self-denying. He heralded the first advent of Christ, and then was not permitted to witness the miracles, and enjoy the power manifested by him. He knew that when Jesus should establish himself as a teacher, he must die. His voice was seldom heard, except in the wilderness. His life was lonely. He did not cling to his father's family, to enjoy their society, but left them in order to fulfill his mission. Multitudes left the busy cities and villages, and flocked to the wilderness to hear the words of the wonderful, singular Prophet. John laid the axe at the root of the tree. He reproved sin fearless of consequences, and prepared the way for the Lamb of God.

Herod was affected as he listened to the powerful, pointed testimonies of John. With deep interest he inquired what he must do to become his disciple. John was acquainted with the fact that he was about to marry his brother's wife, while her husband was yet living, and faithfully told Herod that it was not lawful. Herod was not willing to make any sacrifice. He married his brother's wife, and, through her influence, seized John and put him in prison. But Herod intended to release him again. While there confined, John heard through his disciples of the mighty works of Jesus. He could not listen to his gracious words. But the disciples informed him, and comforted him with what they had heard. Soon John was beheaded through the influence of Herod's wife. I saw that the least disciple that followed Jesus, witnessed his miracles, and heard the comforting words which fell from his lips, was greater than John the Baptist. That is, they were more exalted and honored, and had more pleasure in their lives.

John came in the spirit and power of Elijah, to proclaim the first advent of Jesus. I was pointed down to the last days, and saw that John was to represent those who should go forth in the spirit and power of Elijah, to herald the day of wrath, and the second advent of Jesus.

After the baptism of Jesus in Jordan, he was led by the Spirit into the wilderness, to be tempted of the Devil. The Holy Spirit had fitted him for that special scene of fierce temptations. Forty days he was tempted of the Devil, and in those days he ate nothing. Everything around Jesus was unpleasant, from which human nature would be led to shrink. He was with the wild beasts, and the Devil, in a desolate, lonely place. I saw that the Son of God was pale and emaciated through fasting and suffering. But his course was marked out, and he must fulfill the work he came to do.

Satan took advantage of the sufferings of the Son of God, and prepared to beset him with manifold temptations, hoping he should obtain the victory over him, because he had humbled himself as a man. Satan came with this temptation, If thou be the Son of God, command that this stone be made bread. He tempted Jesus to condescend to him, and give him proof of his being the Messiah, by exercising his divine power. Jesus mildly answered him, It is written, Man shall not live by bread alone, but by every word of God.

Satan was seeking a dispute with Jesus concerning his being the Son of God. He referred to his weak, suffering condition, and boastingly affirmed that he was stronger than Jesus. But the word spoken from heaven, Thou art my beloved Son, in thee I am well pleased, was sufficient to sustain Jesus through all his sufferings. I saw that in all his mission he had nothing to do in convincing Satan of his power, and of his being the Saviour of the world, Satan had sufficient evidence of his exalted station and authority. His unwillingness to yield to Jesus' authority, shut him out of heaven.

Satan, to manifest his strength, carried Jesus to Jerusalem, and set him upon a pinnacle of the temple, and again tempted him, that if he was the Son of God, to give him evidence of it by casting himself down from the dizzy height upon which he had placed him. Satan came with the words of inspiration. For it is written, He shall give his angels charge over thee, and in their hands they shall bear thee up, lest at any time thou dash thy foot against a stone. Jesus answering said unto him, It is said, Thou shalt not tempt the Lord thy God. Satan wished to cause Jesus to presume upon the mercy of his Father, and risk his life before the fulfillment of his mission. He had hoped that the plan of salvation would fail; but I saw that the plan was laid too deep to be thus overthrown, or marred by Satan.

I saw that Christ was the example for all Christians when tempted, or their rights disputed. They should bear it patiently. They should not feel that they have a right to call upon God to display his power, that they may obtain a victory over their enemies, unless there is a special object in view, that God can be directly honored and glorified by it. I saw that if Jesus had cast himself from the pinnacle, it would not have glorified his Father; for none would witness the act but Satan, and the angels of God. And it would be tempting the Lord to display his power to his bitterest foe. It would have been condescending to the one whom Jesus came to conquer.

"And the Devil, taking him up into an high mountain, showed unto him all the kingdoms of the world in a moment of time. And the Devil said unto him, All this power will I give thee, and the glory of them: for that is delivered unto me; and to whomsoever I will I give it. If thou, therefore, wilt worship me, all shall be thine. And Jesus answered and said unto him, Get thee behind me, Satan; for it is written, Thou shalt worship the Lord thy God, and him only shalt thou serve."

Here Satan showed Jesus the kingdoms of the world. They were presented in the most attractive light. He offered them to Jesus if he would there worship him. He told Jesus that he would relinquish his claims of the possessions of earth. Satan knew that his power must be limited, and finally taken away, if the plan of salvation should be carried out. He knew that if Jesus should die to redeem man, his power would end after a season, and he would be destroyed. Therefore it was his studied plan to prevent, if possible, the completion of the great work which had been commenced by the Son of God. If the plan of man's redemption should fail, he would retain the kingdom which he then claimed. And if he should succeed, he flattered himself that he would reign in opposition to the God of heaven.

Satan exulted when Jesus left heaven, and left his power and glory there. He thought that the Son of God was placed in his power. The temptation took so easily with the holy pair in Eden, that he hoped he could with his satanic cunning and power overthrow even the Son of God, and thereby save his life and kingdom. If he could tempt Jesus to depart from the will of his Father, then his object would be gained. Jesus bid Satan get behind him. He was to bow only to his Father. The time was to come when Jesus should redeem the possessions of Satan by his own life, and, after a season, all in heaven and earth should submit to him. Satan claimed the kingdoms of earth as his, and he insinuated to Jesus that all his suffering might be saved. He need not die to obtain the kingdoms of this world. But he might have the entire possessions of earth, and the glory of reigning over them, if he would worship him. Jesus was steadfast. He chose his life of suffering, his dreadful death, and, in the way appointed by his Father, to become a lawful heir to the kingdoms of earth, and have them given into his hands as an everlasting possession. Satan also will be given into his hands to be destroyed by death, never more to annoy Jesus, or the saints in glory.

See Deuteronomy 6:16,8:3; 2Kings 17:35-36; Psalms 91:11-12; Luke chap.2-4

CHAPTER 5

The Ministry of Christ

After Satan had ended his temptations, he departed from Jesus for a season, and angels prepared him food in the wilderness, and strengthened him, and the blessing of his Father rested upon him. Satan had failed in his fiercest temptations, yet he looked forward to the period of Jesus' ministry, when he should at different times try his cunning against him. He still hoped to prevail against him by stirring up those who would not receive Jesus, to hate and seek to destroy him. Satan held a special counsel with his angels. They were disappointed and enraged that they had prevailed nothing against the Son of God. They decided that they must be more cunning, and use their power to the utmost to inspire unbelief in the minds of his own nation as to his being the Saviour of the world, and in this way discourage Jesus in his mission. No matter how exact the Jews might be in their ceremonies and sacrifices, if they could keep their eyes blinded as to the prophecies, and make them believe that it was a mighty, worldly king who was to fulfill these prophecies, they would keep their minds on the stretch for a Messiah to come.

I was then shown that Satan and his angels were very busy during Christ's ministry, inspiring men with unbelief, hate and scorn. Often when Jesus uttered some cutting truth reproving their sins, they would become enraged. Satan and his angels urged them on to take the life of the Son of God. Once they took up stones to cast at him, but angels guarded him, and bore him away from the angry multitude to a place of safety. Again as the plain truth dropped from his holy lips, the multitude laid hold of him, and led him to the brow of a hill, intending to thrust him down. A contention arose among themselves as to what they should do with him, when the angels again hid him from the sight of the multitude, and he, passing through the midst of them, went his way.

Satan still hoped the great plan of salvation would fail. He exerted all his power to make the hearts of all people hard, and their feelings bitter against Jesus. He hoped that the number who would receive him as the Son of God would be so few, that Jesus would consider his sufferings and sacrifice too great to make for so small a company. But I saw that if there had been but two who would have accepted Jesus as the Son of God, to believe in him to the saving of their souls, he would have carried out the plan.

Jesus commenced his work by breaking the power which Satan held over the suffering. He healed those who had suffered by his evil power. He restored the sick to health, healed the lame, and caused them to leap in the gladness of their hearts, and glorify God. He gave sight to the blind, restored to health by his power those who had been infirm and bound by Satan's cruel power many years. The weak, the trembling, and desponding, he comforted with gracious words. He raised the dead to life, and they glorified God for the mighty display of his power. He wrought mightily for all who believed on him. And the feeble suffering ones whom Satan held in triumph, Jesus wrenched from his grasp, and brought to them by his power, soundness of body, and great joy and happiness.

11

The life of Christ was full of benevolence, sympathy and love. He was ever attentive to listen to, and relieve the woes of those who came to him. Multitudes carried the evidences in their own persons of his divine power. Yet many of them soon after the work was accomplished were ashamed of the humble, yet mighty teacher. Because the rulers did not believe on him, they were not willing to suffer with Jesus. He was a man of sorrows and acquainted with grief. But few could endure to be governed by his sober, self-denying life. They wished to enjoy the honor which the world bestows. Many followed the Son of God, and listened to his instructions, feasting upon the words which fell so graciously from his lips. His words were full of meaning, yet so plain that the weakest could understand.

Satan and his angels were busy. They blinded the eyes and darkened the understanding of the Jews. Satan stirred up the chief of the people and the rulers to take his life. They sent officers to bring Jesus unto them, and as they came near where he was, they were greatly amazed. They saw Jesus stirred to sympathy and compassion, as he witnessed human woe. They saw him in love and tenderness speak encouragingly to the weak and afflicted. They also heard him, in a voice of authority, rebuke the power of Satan, and bid the captives held by him, go free. They listened to the words of wisdom that fell from his lips, and they were captivated. They could not lay hands on him. They returned to the priests and elders without Jesus. They inquired of the officers, Why have ye not brought him? They related what they had witnessed of his miracles, and the holy words of wisdom, love and knowledge which they had heard, and ended with saying, Never man spake like this man. The chief priests accused them of being also deceived. Some were ashamed that they had not brought him. The chief priests inquired in a ridiculing manner if any of the rulers had believed on him. I saw that many of the magistrates and elders did believe on Jesus. But Satan kept them from acknowledging it. They feared the reproach of the people more than they feared God.

Thus far the cunning and hatred of Satan had not broken up the plan of salvation. The time for the accomplishment of the object for which Jesus came into the world was drawing on. Satan and his angels consulted together, and decided to inspire Christ's own nation to cry eagerly for his blood, and invent cruelty and scorn to be heaped upon him. He hoped that Jesus would resent such treatment, and not maintain his humility and meekness.

While Satan was laying his plans, Jesus was carefully opening to his disciples the sufferings he must pass through. That he should be crucified, and that he would rise again the third day. But their understanding seemed dull. They could not comprehend what he told them.

See Luke 4:29; John 7:45-48; 8:59

CHAPTER 6

The Transfiguration

I saw that the faith of the disciples was greatly strengthened at the transfiguration. God chose to give the followers of Jesus strong proof that he was the promised Messiah, that in their bitter sorrow and disappointment they should not entirely cast away their confidence. At the transfiguration the Lord sent Moses and Elias to talk with Jesus concerning his suffering and death. Instead of choosing angels to converse with his Son, God chose those who had an experience in the trials of earth. A few of his followers were permitted to be with him and behold his face lighted up with divine glory, and witness his raiment white and glistening, and hear the voice of God, in fearful majesty, saying, This is my beloved Son, hear him.

Elijah had walked with God. His work had not been pleasant. God, through him, had reproved sin. He was a prophet of God, and had to flee from place to place to save his life. He was hunted like the wild beasts that they might destroy him. God translated Elijah. Angels bore him in glory and triumph to heaven.

Moses had been a man greatly honored of God. He was greater than any who had lived before him. He was privileged to talk with God face to face as a man speaketh with a friend. He was permitted to see the bright light and excellent glory that enshrouded the Father. Through Moses the Lord delivered the children of Israel from Egyptian bondage. Moses was a mediator for the children of Israel. He often stood between them and the wrath of God. When the wrath of God was greatly kindled against Israel for their unbelief, their murmurings, and their grievous sins, Moses' love for them was tested. God promised him that if he would let Israel go, let them be destroyed, he would make of him a mighty nation. Moses showed his love for Israel by his earnest pleading. In his distress he prayed God to turn from his fierce anger, and forgive Israel, or blot his name out of his book.

When Israel murmured against God and against Moses, because they could get no water, they accused him of leading them out to kill them and their children. God heard their murmurings, and bade Moses smite the rock, that the children of Israel might have water. Moses smote the rock in wrath, and took the glory to himself. The continual waywardness and murmuring of the children of Israel had caused him the keenest sorrow, and for a little he forgot how much God had borne with them, and that their murmuring was not against Moses, but against God. He thought only of himself, how deeply he was wronged, and how little gratitude they manifested in return, for his deep love for them.

As Moses smote the rock, he failed to honor God, and magnify him before the children of Israel, that they might glorify God. And the Lord was displeased with Moses, and said that he should not enter the promised land. It was God's plan to often prove Israel by bringing them into strait places, and then in their great necessity exhibit his power, that he might live in their memory, and they glorify him.

When Moses came down from the mount with the two tables of stone, and saw Israel worshiping the golden calf, his anger was greatly kindled, and he threw down the tables of stone, and broke them. I saw that Moses did not sin in this. He was wroth for God, jealous for his glory. But when he yielded to the natural feelings of the heart, and took glory to himself, which was due to God, he sinned, and for that sin, God would not suffer him to enter the promised land.

Satan had been trying to find something wherewith to accuse Moses before the angels. Satan triumphed in that he had caused him to displease God, and he exulted, and told the angels that when the Saviour of the world should come to redeem man, he could overcome him. For this transgression Moses came under the power of Satan - the dominion of death. Had he remained steadfast, and not sinned in taking glory to himself, the Lord would have brought him to the promised land, and then translated him to heaven without seeing death.

I saw that Moses passed through death, but Michael came down and gave him life before he saw corruption. Satan claimed the body as his, but Michael resurrected Moses, and took him to heaven. The Devil tried to hold his body, and railed out bitterly against God, denounced him as unjust, in taking from him his prey. But Michael did not rebuke the Devil, although it was through his temptation and power that God's servant had fallen. Christ meekly referred him to his Father, saying, The Lord rebuke thee.

Jesus told his disciples that there were some standing with him who should not taste of death till they should see the kingdom of God come with power. At the transfiguration this promise was fulfilled. The fashion of Jesus' countenance was changed, and shone like the sun. His raiment was white and glistening. Moses was present, and represented those who will be raised from the dead at the second appearing of Jesus. And Elias, who was translated without seeing death, represented those who will be changed to immortality at Christ's second coming, and without seeing death will be translated to heaven. The disciples beheld with fear and astonishment the excellent majesty of Jesus, and the cloud that overshadowed them, and heard the voice of God in terrible majesty, saying, This is my beloved Son, hear him.

See Exodus chap. 32; Numbers 20:7-12; Deuteronomy 34:5; 2 Kings 2:11; Mark chap. 9; Jude 9

CHAPTER 7

The Betrayal of Christ

I was then carried down to the time when Jesus ate the Passover supper with his disciples. Satan had deceived Judas, and led him to think he was one of Christ's true disciples; but his heart had ever been carnal. He had seen the mighty works of Jesus, he had been with him through his ministry, and yielded to the overpowering evidences that he was the Messiah; but he was close and covetous. He loved money. He complained in anger of the costly ointment poured upon Jesus. Mary loved her Lord. He had forgiven her sins which were many, and had raised from the dead her much loved brother, and she felt that nothing was too dear to bestow upon Jesus. The more costly and precious the ointment, the better could Mary express her gratitude to her Saviour, by devoting it to him. Judas, as an excuse for his covetousness, said that the ointment might have been sold and given to the poor. But it was not because he had any care for the poor; for he was selfish, and often appropriated to his own use that which was entrusted to his care to be given to the poor. Judas had not been attentive to the comforts and wants of Jesus, and to excuse his covetousness, he often referred to the poor. And this act of generosity on the part of Mary was a most cutting rebuke of his covetous disposition.

The way was prepared for the temptation of Satan to find a ready reception in Judas' heart. The Jews hated Jesus; but multitudes thronged him to listen to his words of wisdom, and to witness his mighty works. This drew the attention of the people from the chief priests and elders, for the people were stirred with the deepest interest, and anxiously followed Jesus, and listened to the instructions of this wonderful teacher. Many of the chief rulers believed on Jesus, but were afraid to confess it, fearing they would be put out of the synagogue. The priests and elders decided that something must be done to draw the attention of the people from Jesus. They feared that all men would believe on him. They could see no safety for themselves. They must lose their position, or put Jesus to death. And after they should put him to death, there were still those who were living monuments of his power. Jesus had raised Lazarus from the dead. And they feared that if they should kill Jesus, Lazarus would testify of his mighty power. The people were flocking to see him who was raised from the dead, and the rulers determined to slay Lazarus also, and put down the excitement. Then they would turn the people to the traditions and doctrines of men, to tithe mint and rue, and again have influence over them. They agreed to take Jesus when he was alone; for if they should attempt to take him in a crowd, when the minds of the people were all interested in him, they would be stoned.

Judas knew how anxious they were to obtain Jesus, and offered to betray him to the chief priests and elders for a few pieces of silver. His love of money led him to agree to betray his Lord into the hands of his bitterest enemies. Satan was working directly through Judas, and in the midst of the impressive scene of the last supper, he was contriving plans to betray

Jesus. Jesus sorrowfully told his disciples that all of them would be offended because of him, that night. But Peter ardently affirmed that although all should be offended because of him, he would not. Jesus said to Peter, Satan hath desired to have you, that he may sift you as wheat; but I have prayed for thee, that thy faith fail not; and when thou art converted, strengthen thy brethren.

I then viewed Jesus in the garden with his disciples. In deep sorrow he bade them watch and pray lest they should enter into temptation. Jesus knew that their faith was to be tried, and their hopes disappointed, and that they would need all the strength they could obtain by close watching and fervent prayer. With strong cries and weeping, Jesus prayed, Father, if thou be willing, remove this cup from me, nevertheless, not my will, but thine be done. The Son of God prayed in agony. Large drops of sweat like blood came out of his face, and fell upon the ground. Angels were hovering over the place, witnessing the scene, while only one was commissioned to go and strengthen the Son of God in his agony. The angels in heaven cast their crowns and harps from them, and with the deepest interest silently watched Jesus. There was no joy in heaven. They wished to surround the Son of God, but the commanding angels suffered them not, lest, as they should behold his betrayal, they would deliver him; for the plan was laid out, and it must be fulfilled.

After Jesus had prayed, he came to see his disciples. They were sleeping. He had not the comfort and prayers of even his disciples in that dreadful hour. Peter who was so zealous a little before, was heavy with sleep. Jesus reminded him of his positive declarations, and said unto him, What! could ye not watch with me one hour? Three times the Son of God prayed in agony, when Judas, with his band of men, was at hand. He met Jesus as usual to salute him. The band surrounded Jesus; but there he manifested his divine power, as he said, Whom seek ye? I am he. They fell backward to the ground. Jesus made this inquiry that they might witness his power, and have evidence that he could deliver himself from their hands if he would.

The disciples began to hope as they saw the multitude with their staves and swords fall so quickly. As they arose and again surrounded the Son of God, Peter drew the sword and cut off an ear. Jesus bid him put up the sword, and said unto him, Thinkest thou that I cannot now pray to my Father, and he shall presently give me more than twelve legions of angels? I saw that as these words were spoken, the countenances of the angels were animated. They wished then, and there, to surround their commander, and disperse that angry mob. But again sadness settled upon them as Jesus added, But how then shall the scriptures be fulfilled, that thus it must be? The hearts of the disciples sunk again in despair and bitter disappointment, as Jesus suffered them to lead him away.

The disciples were afraid of their own lives, and fled one this way, and the other that, and Jesus was left alone. O what triumph of Satan then! And what sadness and sorrow with the angels of God! Many companies of holy angels, with each a tall commanding angel at their head, were sent to witness the scene. They were to record every act, every insult and cruelty imposed upon the Son of God, and to register every pang of anguish which Jesus should suffer; for the very men should see it all again in living characters.

See Matthew 26:1-56; Mark 14:1-52; Luke 22:1-46; John chap.11, 12:1-11, 18:1-12

CHAPTER 8

The Trial of Christ

The angels as they left heaven, in sadness laid off their glittering crowns. They could not wear them while their commander was suffering, and was to wear a crown of thorns. Satan and his angels were busy in that judgment hall to destroy humanity and sympathy. The very atmosphere was heavy and polluted by their influence. The chief priests and elders were inspired by them to abuse and insult Jesus, in a manner the most difficult for human nature to bear. Satan hoped that such insult and sufferings would call forth from the Son of God some complaint or murmur; or that he would manifest his divine power, and wrench himself from the grasp of the multitude, and thus the plan of salvation at last fail.

Peter followed his Lord after his betrayal. He was anxious to see what would be done with Jesus. And when he was accused of being one of his disciples, he denied it. He was afraid of his life, and when charged with being one of them, he declared that he knew not the man. The disciples were noted for the purity of their words, and Peter, to deceive, and convince them that he was not one of Christ's disciples, denied it the third time with cursing and swearing. Jesus, who was some distance from Peter, turned a sorrowful reproving gaze upon him. Then he remembered the words which Jesus had spoken to him in the upper chamber, and also his zealous assertion, Though all men shall be offended because of thee, yet will I never be offended. He denied his Lord, even with cursing and swearing; but that look of Jesus melted Peter at once, and saved him. He bitterly wept and repented of his great sin, and was converted, and then was prepared to strengthen his brethren.

The multitude were clamorous for the blood of Jesus. They cruelly scourged him, and put an old purple, kingly robe upon him, and bound his sacred head with a crown of thorns. They put a reed in his hand, and mockingly bowed to him, and saluted him with, Hail king of the Jews! They then took the reed from his hand, and smote him with it upon the head, causing the thorns to penetrate his temples, sending the trickling blood down his face and beard.

It was difficult for the angels to endure the sight. They would have delivered Jesus out of their hands; but the commanding angels forbade them, and said that it was a great ransom that was to be paid for man; but it would be complete, and would cause the death of him who had the power of death. Jesus knew that angels were witnessing the scene of his humiliation. I saw that the feeblest angel could have caused that multitude to fall powerless, and delivered Jesus. He knew that if he should desire it of his Father, angels would instantly release him. But it was necessary that Jesus should suffer many things of wicked men, in order to carry out the plan of salvation.

There stood Jesus, meek and humble before the infuriated multitude, while they offered him the meanest abuse. They spit in his face - that face which they will one day desire to be hid from, which will give light to the city of God, and shine brighter than the sun -- but not an angry look did he cast upon the offenders. He meekly raised his hand, and wiped it off. They covered his head with an old garment; blindfolded him, and then struck him in the face, and cried out, Prophesy unto us who it was that smote thee. There was commotion among the angels. They would have rescued him instantly; but their commanding angel restrained them.

The disciples had gained confidence to enter where Jesus was, and witness his trial. They expected that he would manifest his divine power, and deliver himself from the hands of his enemies, and punish them for their cruelty towards him. Their hopes would rise and fall as the different scenes transpired. Sometimes they doubted, and feared they had been deceived. But the voice heard at the mount of transfiguration, and the glory they there witnessed, strengthened them that he was the Son of God. They called to mind the exciting scenes which they had witnessed, the miracles they had seen Jesus do in healing the sick, opening the eyes of the blind, unstopping the deaf ears, rebuking and casting out devils, raising the dead to life, and even rebuking the wind, and it obeyed him. They could not believe that he would die. They hoped he would yet rise in power, and with his commanding voice disperse that blood-thirsty multitude, as when he entered the temple and drove out those who were making the house of God a place of merchandise; when they fled before him, as though a company of armed soldiers were pursuing them. The disciples hoped that Jesus would manifest his power, and convince all that he was the King of Israel.

Judas was filled with bitter remorse and shame at his treacherous act in betraying Jesus. And when he witnessed the abuse he suffered, he was overcome. He had loved Jesus, but loved money more. He did not think that Jesus would suffer himself to be taken by the mob which he had led on. He thought that Jesus would work a miracle, and deliver himself from them. But when he saw the infuriated multitude in the judgment hall, thirsting for his blood, he deeply felt his guilt, and while many were vehemently accusing Jesus, Judas rushed through the multitude, confessing that he had sinned in betraying innocent blood. He offered them the money, and begged of them to release Jesus, declaring that he was entirely innocent. Vexation and confusion kept the priests for a short time silent. They did not wish the people to know that they had hired one of Jesus' professed followers to betray him into their hands. Their hunting Jesus like a thief and taking him secretly, they wished to hide. But the confession of Judas, his haggard and guilty appearance, exposed the priests before the multitude, showing that it was hatred that had caused them to take Jesus. As Judas loudly declared Jesus to be innocent, the priests replied, What is that to us? See thou to that. They had Jesus in their power, and they were determined to make sure of him. Judas, overwhelmed with anguish, threw the money that he now despised at the feet of those who had hired him, and in anguish and horror at his crime, went and hung himself.

Jesus had many sympathizers in that company, and his answering nothing to the many questions put to him amazed the throng. To all the insults and mockery not a frown, not a troubled expression was upon his features. He was dignified and composed. He was of perfect and noble form. The spectators looked upon him with wonder. They compared his perfect form, his firm, dignified bearing, with those who sat in judgment against him, and said to one another that he appeared more like a king to be entrusted with a kingdom than any of the rulers. He bore no marks of being a criminal. His eye was mild, clear and undaunted, his forehead broad and high. Every feature was strongly marked with benevolence and noble principle. His patience and forbearance were so unlike man, that many trembled. Even Herod and Pilate were greatly troubled at his noble, God-like bearing.

Pilate from the first was convicted that he was no common man, but an excellent character. He believed him to be entirely innocent. The angels who were witnessing the whole scene noticed the convictions of Pilate, and marked his sympathy and compassion for Jesus; and to save him from engaging in the awful act of delivering Jesus to be crucified, an angel was sent to Pilate's wife, and gave her information through a dream that it was the Son of God in whose trial Pilate was engaged, and that he was an innocent sufferer. She immediately sent word to Pilate that she had suffered many things in a dream on account of Jesus, and warned him to have nothing to do with that holy man. The messenger bearing the communication pressed hastily through the crowd, and handed it to Pilate. As he read it he trembled and turned pale. He at once thought he would have nothing to do in the matter; that if they would have the blood of Jesus he would not give his influence to it, but would labor to deliver him.

When Pilate heard that Herod was at Jerusalem he was glad, and hoped to free himself from the disagreeable matter altogether, and have nothing to do in condemning Jesus. He sent him, with his accusers, to Herod. Herod was hardened. His murdering John left a stain upon his conscience which he could not free himself from, and when he heard of Jesus, and the mighty works done by him, he thought it was John risen from the dead. He feared and trembled, for he bore a guilty conscience. Jesus was placed in Herod's hands by Pilate. Herod considered this act an acknowledgment from Pilate of his power, authority and judgment. They had previously been enemies, but then they were made friends. Herod was glad to see Jesus, for he expected that he would work some mighty miracle for his satisfaction. But it was not the work of Jesus to gratify his curiosity. His divine and miraculous power was to be exercised for the salvation of others, but not in his own behalf.

Jesus answered nothing to the many questions put to him by Herod; neither did he regard his enemies who were vehemently accusing him. Herod was enraged because Jesus did not appear to fear his power, and with his men of war, derided, mocked and abused the Son of God. Herod was astonished at the noble, God-like appearance of Jesus, when shamefully abused, and feared to condemn him, and he sent him again to Pilate.

Satan and his angels were tempting Pilate, and trying to lead him on to his own ruin. They suggested to him that if he did not take any part in condemning Jesus, others would; the multitude were thirsting for his blood; and if he did not deliver Jesus to be crucified, he would lose his power and worldly honor, and would be denounced as a believer on the impostor, as they termed him. Pilate, through fear of losing his power and authority, consented to the death of Jesus. And notwithstanding he placed the blood of Jesus upon his accusers, and the multitude received it, crying, His blood be on us and on our children, yet

Pilate was not clear; he was guilty of the blood of Christ. For his own selfish interest, and love of honor from the great men of earth, he delivered an innocent man to die. If Pilate had followed his conviction, he would have had nothing to do with condemning Jesus.

The trial and condemnation of Jesus were working on the minds of many; and impressions were being made which were to appear after his resurrection; and many were to be added to the Church whose experience and conviction should be dated from the time of Jesus' trial.

Satan's rage was great as he saw that all the cruelty which he had led the chief priests to inflict on Jesus had not called forth from him the least murmur. I saw that, although Jesus had taken man's nature, a power and fortitude that was God-like sustained him, and he did not depart from the will of his Father in the least.

See Matthew 26:57-75, 27:1-31; Mark 14:53-72, 15:1-20; Luke 22:47-71, 23:1-25; John chap.18, 19:1-16

CHAPTER 9

The Crucifixion of Christ

The Son of God was delivered to the people to be crucified. They led the dear Saviour away. He was weak and feeble through pain and suffering, caused by the scourging and blows which he had received, yet they laid on him the heavy cross upon which they were soon to nail him. But Jesus fainted beneath the burden. Three times they laid on him the heavy cross, and three times he fainted. They then seized one of his followers, a man who had not openly professed faith in Christ, yet believed on him. They laid on him the cross, and he bore it to the fatal spot. Companies of angels were marshaled in the air above the place. A number of his disciples followed him to Calvary in sorrow, and with bitter weeping. They called to mind Jesus' riding triumphantly into Jerusalem, and they following him, crying, Hosanna in the highest! and strewing their garments in the way, and the beautiful palm branches. They thought that he was then to take the kingdom and reign a temporal prince over Israel. How changed the scene! How blighted their prospects! They followed Jesus; not with rejoicing; not with bounding hearts and cheerful hopes; but with hearts stricken with fear and despair they slowly, sadly followed him who had been disgraced and humbled, and who was about to die.

The mother of Jesus was there. Her heart was pierced with anguish, such as none but a fond mother can feel. Her stricken heart still hoped, with the disciples, that her Son would work some mighty miracle, and deliver himself from his murderers. She could not endure the thought that he would suffer himself to be crucified. But the preparations were made, and they laid Jesus upon the cross. The hammer and the nails were brought. The heart of his disciples fainted within them. The mother of Jesus was agonized, almost beyond endurance, and as they stretched Jesus upon the cross, and were about to fasten his hands with the cruel nails to the wooden arms, the disciples bore the mother of Jesus from the scene, that she might not hear the crashing of the nails, as they were driven through the bone and muscle of his tender hands and feet. Jesus murmured not; but groaned in agony. His face was pale, and large drops of sweat stood upon his brow. Satan exulted in the sufferings which the Son of God was passing through, yet feared that his kingdom was lost, and that he must die.

They raised the cross after they had nailed Jesus to it, and with great force thrust it into the place prepared for it in the ground, tearing the flesh, and causing the most intense suffering. They made his death as shameful as possible. With him they crucified two thieves, one on either side of Jesus. The thieves were taken by force, and after much resistance on their part, their arms were thrust back and nailed to their crosses. But Jesus meekly submitted. He needed no one to force his arms back upon the cross. While the thieves were cursing their executioners, Jesus in agony prayed for his enemies, Father, forgive them, for they know not what they do. It was not merely agony of body which Jesus endured, but the sins of the whole world were upon him.

As Jesus hung upon the cross, some who passed by reviled him, wagging their heads, as though bowing to a king, and said to him, Thou that destroyest the temple and buildest it in three days, save thyself. If thou be the Son of God, come down from the cross. The Devil used the same words to Christ in the wilderness, If thou be the Son of God. The chief priests and elders and scribes mockingly said, He saved others, himself he cannot save. If he be the King of Israel, let him now come down from the cross, and we will believe him. The angels who hovered over the scene of Christ's crucifixion were moved to indignation as the rulers derided him, and said, If he be the Son of God let him deliver himself. They wished there to come to the rescue of Jesus, and deliver him; but they were not suffered to do so. The object of his mission was almost accomplished. As Jesus hung upon the cross those dreadful hours of agony, he did not forget his mother. She could not remain away from the suffering scene. Jesus' last lesson was one of compassion and humanity. He looked upon his mother, whose heart was well nigh bursting with grief, and then upon his beloved disciple John. He said to his mother, Woman, behold thy Son. Then said he to John, Behold thy mother. And from that hour John took her to his own house.

Jesus thirsted in his agony; but they heaped upon him additional insult, by giving him vinegar and gall to drink. The angels had viewed the horrid scene of the crucifixion of their loved commander, until they could behold no longer; and veiled their faces from the sight. The sun refused to look upon the dreadful scene. Jesus cried with a loud voice, which struck terror to the hearts of his murderers, *It is finished*. Then the veil of the temple was rent from the top to the bottom, the earth shook, and the rocks rent. Great darkness was upon the face of the earth. The last hope of the disciples seemed swept away as Jesus died. Many of his followers witnessed the scene of his sufferings and death, and their cup of sorrow was full.

Satan did not then exult as he had done. He had hoped that he could break up the plan of salvation; but it was laid too deep. And now by Jesus' death, he knew that he must finally die, and his kingdom be taken away and given to Jesus. He held a council with his angels. He had prevailed nothing against the Son of God, and now they must increase their efforts, and with their cunning and power turn to Jesus' followers. They must prevent all they could from receiving salvation purchased for them by Jesus. By so doing Satan could still work against the government of God. Also it would be for his own interest to keep from Jesus all he could. For the sins of those who are redeemed by the blood of Christ, and overcome, at last will be rolled back upon the originator of sin, the Devil, and he will have to bear their sins, while those who do not accept salvation through Jesus will bear their own sins.

Jesus' life was without worldly grandeur, or extravagant show. His humble, self-denying life was a great contrast to the lives of the priests and elders, who loved ease and worldly honor, and the strict and holy life of Jesus was a continual reproof to them, on account of their sins. They despised him for his humbleness, and purity. But those who despised him here, will one day see him in the grandeur of heaven, and the unsurpassed glory of his Father. He was surrounded with enemies in the judgment hall, who were thirsting for his blood; but those hardened ones who cried out, His blood be on us and on our children, will behold him an honored King. All the heavenly host will escort him on his way with songs of victory, majesty and might, to him that was slain, yet lives again a mighty conqueror. Poor, weak, miserable man spit in the face of the King of glory, while a shout of brutal triumph arose from the mob at the degrading insult. They marred that face with blows and cruelty which filled all heaven with admiration. They will behold that face again, bright as the noonday sun, and will seek to flee from before it. Instead of that shout of brutal triumph, in terror they will wail because of him. Jesus will present his hands with the marks of his crucifixion. The marks of this cruelty he will ever bear. Every print of the nails will tell the story of man's wonderful redemption, and the dear price that purchased it. The very men who thrust the spear into the side of the Lord of life, will behold the print of the spear, and will lament with deep anguish the part they acted in marring his body. His murderers were greatly annoyed by the superscription, **The King of the Jews**, placed upon the cross above his head. But then they will be obliged to see him in all his glory and kingly power. They will behold on his vesture and on his thigh, written in living characters, **King of Kings, and Lord of Lords**. They cried to him mockingly, as he hung upon the cross, Let Christ the King of Israel descend from the cross, that we may see and believe. They will behold him then with kingly power and authority. They will demand no evidence then of his being the King of Israel; but overwhelmed with a sense of his majesty and exceeding glory, they will be compelled to acknowledge, Blessed is he that cometh in the name of the Lord.

The shaking of the earth, the rending of the rocks, the darkness spread over the earth, and the loud, strong cry of Jesus, *It is finished*, as he yielded up his life, troubled his enemies, and made his murderers tremble. The disciples wondered at these singular manifestations; but their hopes were all crushed. They were afraid the Jews would seek to destroy them also. Such hate manifested against the Son of God they thought would not end there. Lonely hours the disciples spent in sorrow, weeping over their disappointment. They expected that he would reign a temporal prince; but their hopes died with Jesus. They doubted in their sorrow and disappointment whether Jesus had not deceived them. His mother was humbled, and even her faith wavered in his being the Messiah.

But notwithstanding the disciples had been disappointed in their hopes concerning Jesus, yet they loved him, and respected and honored his body, but knew not how to obtain it. Joseph of Arimathea, an honorable counsellor, had influence, and was one of Jesus' true disciples. He went privately, yet boldly, to Pilate and begged his body. He dared not go openly; for the hatred of the Jews was so great that the disciples feared that an effort would be made by them to prevent the body of Jesus having an honored resting place. But Pilate granted his request, and as they took the body of Jesus down from the cross, their sorrows were renewed, and they mourned over their blighted hopes in deep anguish. They wrapped Jesus in fine linen, and Joseph laid him in his own new sepulchre. The women who had been his humble followers while he lived still kept near him after his death, and would not leave him until they saw his sacred body laid in the sepulchre, and a stone of great weight rolled at the door, lest his enemies should seek to obtain his body. But they need not have feared; for I beheld the angelic host watching with untold interest the resting place of Jesus. They guarded the sepulchre, earnestly waiting the command to act their part in liberating the King of glory from his prison house.

Christ's murderers were afraid that he might yet come to life and escape them. They begged of Pilate a watch to guard the sepulchre until the third day. Pilate granted them armed soldiers to guard the sepulchre, sealing the stone at the door, lest his disciples should steal him away, and say that he had risen from the dead.

See Matthew 21:1-11, 27:32-66; Mark 15:21-47; Luke 23:26-56; John 19:17-42; Revelation 19:11-16

CHAPTER 10

The Resurrection of Christ

The disciples rested on the Sabbath, sorrowing for the death of their Lord, while Jesus, the King of glory, rested in the sepulchre. The night had worn slowly away, and while it was yet dark, the angels hovering over the sepulchre knew that the time of the release of God's dear Son, their loved commander, had nearly come. And as they were waiting with the deepest emotion the hour of his triumph, a strong and mighty angel came flying swiftly from heaven. His face was like the lightning, and his garments white as snow. His light dispersed the darkness from his track, and caused the evil angels who had triumphantly claimed the body of Jesus, to flee in terror from his brightness and glory. One of the angelic host who had witnessed the scene of Jesus' humiliation, and was watching his sacred resting place, joined the angel from heaven, and together they came down to the sepulchre. The earth shook and trembled as they approached, and there was a mighty earthquake. The strong and mighty angel laid hold of the stone and quickly rolled it away from the door of the sepulchre, and sat upon it.

Terrible fear seized the guard. Where was now their power to keep the body of Jesus? They did not think of their duty, or of the disciples stealing him away. They were amazed and affrighted, as the exceeding bright light of the angels shone all around brighter than the sun. The Roman guard saw the angels, and fell as dead men to the ground. One angel rolled back the stone in triumph, and with a clear and mighty voice, cried out, Thou Son of God! Thy Father calls thee! Come forth! Death could hold dominion over him no longer. Jesus arose from the dead. The other angel entered the sepulchre, and as Jesus arose in triumph, he unbound the napkin which was about his head, and Jesus walked forth a victorious conqueror. In solemn awe the angelic host gazed upon the scene. And as Jesus walked forth from the sepulchre in majesty, those shining angels prostrated themselves to the ground and worshiped him; then hailed him with songs of victory and triumph, that death could hold its divine captive no longer. Satan did not now triumph. His angels had fled before the bright, penetrating light of the heavenly angels. They bitterly complained to their king, that their prey had been taken violently from them, and that he whom they so much hated had risen from the dead.

Satan and his angels had enjoyed a little moment of triumph that their power over fallen man had caused the Lord of life, to be laid in the grave; but short was their hellish triumph. For as Jesus walked forth from his prison house a majestic conqueror, Satan knew that after a season he must die, and his kingdom pass unto him whose right it was. He lamented and raged that notwithstanding all his efforts and power, Jesus had not been overcome, but had laid open a way of salvation for man, and whosoever would, might walk in it and be saved.

For a little, Satan seemed sad and showed distress. He held a council with his angels to consider what they should engage in next to work against the government of God. Said Satan, You must hasten to the chief priests and elders. We succeeded in deceiving them and blinding their eyes, and hardening their hearts against Jesus. We made them believe he was an impostor. That Roman guard will carry the hateful news that Christ is risen. We led the priests and elders on to hate Jesus, and to murder him. Now hold it before them in a bright light, that as they were his murderers, if it becomes known that Jesus is risen, they will be stoned to death by the people, in that they killed an innocent man.

I saw the Roman guard, as the angelic host passed back to heaven, and the light and glory passed away, raise themselves to see if it were safe for them to look around. They were filled with amazement as they saw that the great stone was rolled from the door of the sepulchre, and Jesus was risen. They hastened to the chief priests and elders with the wonderful story of what they had seen; and as those murderers heard the marvelous report, paleness sat upon every face. Horror seized them at what they had done. They then realized that if the report was correct, they were lost. For a little they were stupefied, and looked one to the other in silence, not knowing what to do or say. They were placed where they could not believe unless it be to their own condemnation. They went aside by themselves to consult what should be done. They decided that if it should be spread abroad that Jesus had risen, and the report of such amazing glory, which caused the guard to fall like dead men, should come to the people, they would surely be enraged, and would slay them. They decided to hire the soldiers to keep the matter secret. They offered them much money, saying, Say ye, His disciples came by night and stole him away while we slept. And when the guard inquired what should be done with them for sleeping at their post, the priests and elders said that they would persuade the governor and save them. For the sake of money the Roman guard sold their honor, and agreed to follow the counsel of the priests and elders.

When Jesus as he hung upon the cross, cried out, *It is finished,* the rocks rent, the earth shook, and some of the graves were shaken open; for when Jesus arose from the dead, and conquered death and the grave; when he walked forth from his prison house a triumphant conqueror; while the earth was reeling and shaking, and the excellent glory of heaven clustered around the sacred spot, obedient to his call, many of the righteous dead came forth as witnesses that he had risen. Those favored, resurrected saints came forth glorified. They were a few chosen and holy ones who had lived in every age from creation, even down to the days of Christ. And while the chief priests and Pharisees were seeking to cover up the resurrection of Christ, God chose to bring up a company from their graves to testify that Jesus had risen, and to declare his glory.

Those who were resurrected were of different stature and form. I was informed that the inhabitants of earth had been degenerating, losing their strength and comeliness. Satan has the power of disease and death, and in every age the curse has been more visible, and the power of Satan more plainly seen. Some of those raised were more noble in appearance and form than others. I was informed that those who lived in the days of Noah and Abraham were more like the angels in form, in comeliness and strength. But every generation has been growing weaker, and more subject to disease, and their lives of shorter duration. Satan has been learning how to annoy men, and enfeeble the race.

Those holy ones who came forth after the resurrection of Jesus appeared unto many, telling them that the sacrifice for man was completed, that Jesus, whom the Jews crucified, had risen from the dead, and added, We be risen with him. They bore testimony that it was by his mighty power that they had been called forth from their graves. Notwithstanding the lying reports circulated, the matter could not be concealed by Satan, his angels, or the chief priests; for this holy company, brought forth from their graves, spread the wonderful, joyful news; also Jesus showed himself unto his sorrowing, heart-broken disciples, dispelling their fears, and causing them gladness and joy.

As the news spread from city to city, and from town to town, the Jews in their turn were afraid for their lives, and concealed the hate they cherished towards the disciples. Their only hope was to spread their lying report. And those who wished this lie to be true, believed it. Pilate trembled. He believed the strong testimony given, that Jesus was risen from the dead, and that many others he had brought up with him, and his peace left him forever. For the sake of worldly honor; for fear of losing his authority, and his life, he delivered Jesus to die. He was now fully convinced that it was not merely a common, innocent man of whose blood he was guilty but the blood of the Son of God. Miserable was the life of Pilate; miserable to its close. Despair and anguish crushed every hopeful, joyful feeling. He refused to be comforted, and died a most miserable death.

Herod's heart grew still harder, and when he heard that Jesus had arisen, he was not much troubled. He took the life of James; and when he saw that this pleased the Jews, he took Peter also, intending to put him to death. But God had a work for Peter to do, and sent his angel and delivered him. Herod was visited with judgment. God smote him in the sight of a great multitude as he was exalting himself before them, and he died a horrible death.

Early in the morning before it was yet light, the holy women came to the sepulchre, bringing sweet spices to anoint the body of Jesus, when lo! they found the heavy stone rolled away from the door of the sepulchre, and the body of Jesus was not there. Their hearts sunk within them, and they feared that their enemies had taken away the body. And, behold, two angels in white apparel stood by them; their faces were bright and shining. They understood the errand of the holy women, and immediately told them that they were seeking Jesus, but he was not there, he had risen, and they could behold the place where he lay. They bid them go tell his disciples that he would go before them into Galilee. But the women were frightened and astonished. They hastily ran to the disciples who were mourning, and could not be comforted because their Lord had been crucified; they hurriedly told them the things which they had seen and heard. The disciples could not believe that he had risen, but, with the women who had brought the report, ran hastily to the sepulchre, and found that truly Jesus was not there. There were his linen clothes, but they could not believe the good news that Jesus had risen from the dead. They returned home marveling at the things they had seen, also at the report brought them by the women. But Mary chose to linger around the sepulchre, thinking of what she had seen, and distressed with the thought that she might have been deceived. She felt that new trials awaited her. Her grief was renewed, and she broke forth in bitter weeping. She stooped down to look again into the sepulchre, and beheld two angels clothed in white. Their countenances were bright and shining. One was sitting at the head, the other at the feet, where Jesus had lain. They spoke to her tenderly, and asked her why she wept. She replied, They have taken away my Lord, and I know not where they have laid him.

And as she turned from the sepulchre, she saw Jesus standing by her; but knew him not. Jesus spoke tenderly to Mary, and inquired the cause of her sorrow, and asked her whom she was seeking. She supposed he was the gardener, and begged of him, if he had borne away her Lord, to tell her where he had laid him, and she would take him away. Jesus spoke to her with his own heavenly voice, and said, Mary. She was acquainted with the tones of that dear voice, and quickly answered, Master! and with joy and gladness was about to embrace him; but Jesus stood back, and said, Touch me not, for I am not yet ascended to my Father; but go to my brethren and say unto them, I ascend unto my Father, and your Father, and to my God, and your God. Joyfully she hastened to the disciples with the good news. Jesus quickly ascended up to his Father to bear from his lips that he accepted the sacrifice, and that he had done all things well, and to receive all power in heaven, and upon earth, from his Father.

Angels like a cloud surrounded the Son of God, and bid the everlasting gates to be lifted up, that the King of glory might come in. I saw that while Jesus was with that bright, heavenly host, and in the presence of his Father, and the glory of God surrounded him, he did not forget his poor disciples upon earth; but received power from his Father, that he might return unto them, and while with them impart power unto them. The same day he returned, and showed himself to his disciples. He suffered them then to touch him, for he had ascended to his Father, and had received power.

But at this time Thomas was not present. He would not humbly receive the report of the disciples; but firmly, and self-confidently affirmed that he would not believe, unless he should put his fingers in the prints of the nails, and his hand in his side where the cruel spear was thrust. In this he showed a lack of confidence in his brethren. And if all should require the same evidence, but few would receive Jesus, and believe in his resurrection. But it was the will of God that the report of the disciples should go from one to the other, and many receive it from the lips of those who had seen and heard. God was not well pleased with such unbelief. And when Jesus met with his disciples again, Thomas was with them. The moment he beheld Jesus he believed. But he had declared that he would not be satisfied without the evidence of feeling added to sight, and Jesus gave him the evidence he had desired. Thomas cried out, my Lord and my God. But Jesus reproved Thomas for his unbelief. He said to him, Thomas, because thou hast seen me, thou hast believed; blessed are they that have not seen and yet have believed.

So, I saw, that those who had no experience in the first and second angels' messages 1 must receive them from those who had an experience, and followed down through the messages. As Jesus was crucified, so I saw that these messages have been crucified. And as the disciples declared that there was salvation in no other name under heaven, given among men; so, also, should the servants of God faithfully and fearlessly declare that those who embrace but a part of the truths connected with the third message 2 must gladly embrace the first, second and third messages as God has given them, or have no part nor lot in the matter.

I was shown that while the holy women were carrying the report that Jesus had risen, the Roman guard were circulating the lie that had been put in their mouths by the chief priests and elders, that the disciples came by night, while they slept, and stole the body of Jesus. Satan had put this lie into the hearts and mouths of the chief priests, and the people stood ready to receive their word. But God had made this matter sure, and placed this important event, upon which hangs salvation, beyond all doubt, and where it was impossible for priests and elders to cover it up. Witnesses were raised from the dead to testify to Christ's resurrection.

Jesus remained with his disciples forty days, causing them joy and gladness of heart, and opening to them more fully the realities of the kingdom of God. He commissioned them to bear testimony to the things which they had seen and heard, concerning his sufferings, death and resurrection; that he had made a sacrifice for sin, that all who would, might come unto him and find life. He with faithful tenderness told them that they would be persecuted and distressed; but they would find relief in referring to their experience, and remembering the words he had spoken to them. He told them that he had overcome the temptations of the Devil, and maintained the victory through trials and suffering, that Satan could have no more power over him, but would more directly bring his temptations and power to bear upon them, and upon all who should believe in his name. He told them that they could overcome, as he had overcome. Jesus endowed his disciples with power to do miracles, and he told them that although wicked men should have power over their bodies, he would at certain times send his angels and deliver them; that their lives could not be taken from them until their mission should be accomplished. And when their testimony should be finished, their lives might be required to seal the testimonies which they had borne. His anxious followers gladly listened to his teachings. They eagerly feasted upon every word which fell from his holy lips. Then they certainly knew that he was the Saviour of the world. Every word sunk with deep weight into their hearts, and they sorrowed that they must be parted from their blessed, heavenly teacher; that after a little they should no more hear comforting, gracious words from his lips. But again their hearts were warmed with love and exceeding joy, as Jesus told them that he would go and prepare mansions for them, and come again and receive them, that they might ever be with him. He told them that he would send them the Comforter, the Holy Spirit, to guide, bless and lead them into all truth; and he lifted up his hands and blessed them.

Footnotes

<u>1</u> See Revelation 14:6-8. Explained in chapters 23 and 24 of this book.

<u>2</u> See Revelation 14:9-12. Explained in chapter 28 of this book.

See Matthew 27:52-53, chap. 28; Mark 16:1-18; Luke 24:1-50; John chap. 20; Acts chap. 12.

CHAPTER 11

The Ascension of Christ

All heaven was waiting the hour of triumph when Jesus should ascend to his Father. Angels came to receive the King of glory, and to escort him triumphantly to heaven. After Jesus had blessed his disciples, he was parted from them, and taken up. And as he led the way upward, the multitude of captives who were raised at his resurrection followed. A multitude of the heavenly host was in attendance; while in heaven an innumerable number of angels awaited his coming. As they ascended up to the holy city, the angels who escorted Jesus cried out, Lift up your heads, O ye gates, and be ye lift up, ye everlasting doors, and the King of glory shall come in. With rapture the angels in the city, who awaited his coming, cried out, who is this King of glory? The escorting angels with triumph answered, The Lord strong and mighty! The Lord mighty in battle! Lift up your heads, O ye gates! even lift them up, ye everlasting doors, and the King of glory shall come in. Again the heavenly host cried out, Who is this King of glory? The escorting angels in melodious strains answered, The Lord of hosts! He is the King of Glory! And the heavenly train passed into the city. Then all the heavenly host surrounded the Son of God, their majestic commander, and with the deepest adoration bowed, casting their glittering crowns at his feet. And then they touched their golden harps, and in sweet, melodious strains, filled all heaven with their rich music and songs to the Lamb who was slain, yet lives again in majesty and glory.

Next I was shown the disciples as they sorrowfully gazed towards heaven to catch the last glimpse of their ascending Lord. Two angels clothed in white apparel stood by them, and said unto them, Ye men of Galilee, why stand ye gazing up into heaven? This same Jesus, which is taken up from you into heaven, shall so come in like manner as ye have seen him go into heaven. The disciples, with the mother of Jesus, witnessed the ascension of the Son of God, and they spent that night in talking over his wonderful acts, and the strange and glorious things which had transpired within a short time.

Satan counselled with his angels, and with bitter hatred against God's government, told them that while he retained his power and authority upon earth, their efforts must be tenfold stronger against the followers of Jesus. They had prevailed nothing against Jesus; but his followers they must overthrow if possible, and carry on his work through every generation, to ensnare those who should believe in Jesus, his resurrection and ascension. Satan related to his angels that Jesus had given his disciples power to cast them out, rebuke them, and heal those whom he should afflict. Then Satan's angels went forth like roaring lions, seeking to destroy the followers of Jesus.

See Psalms 24:7-10, Acts1:1-11

CHAPTER 12

The Disciples of Christ

With mighty power the disciples preached a crucified and a risen Savior. They healed the sick, even one who had always been lame was restored to perfect soundness, and entered with them into the temple, walking and leaping and praising God in the sight of all the people. The news spread, and the people began to press around the disciples. Many ran together, greatly astonished and amazed at the cure that had been wrought.

When Jesus died the chief priests thought that there would be no more miracles wrought among them, that the excitement would die, and that the people would again turn to the traditions of men. But, lo! right in their midst, the disciples were working miracles, and the people were filled with amazement, and gazed with wonder upon them. Jesus had been crucified, and they wondered where the disciples had obtained this power. When he was alive they thought that he imparted power to his disciples; when Jesus died, they expected those miracles would end. Peter understood their perplexity, and said to them, Ye men of Israel, why marvel ye at this? or why look ye so earnestly on us, as though by our own power or holiness we had made this man to walk? The God of Abraham, and of Isaac, and of Jacob, the God of our fathers hath glorified his Son Jesus, whom ye delivered up, and denied him in the presence of Pilate, when he was determined to let him go. But ye denied the Holy One, and the Just, and desired a murderer to be granted unto you, and killed the Prince of life, whom God hath raised from the dead, whereof we are witnesses. Peter told them that it was faith in Jesus that had caused this perfect soundness of a man who was before a cripple.

The chief priests and elders could not bear these words. They laid hold of the disciples and put them in confinement. But thousands were converted, and believed in the resurrection and ascension of Christ, by hearing only one discourse from the disciples. The chief priests and elders were troubled. They had slain Jesus that the minds of the people might be turned to themselves; but the matter was now worse than before. They were openly accused by the disciples of being the murderers of the Son of God, and they could not determine to what extent these things might grow, or how they themselves would be regarded by the people. They would gladly have put the disciples to death; but dared not for fear the people would stone them. They called for the disciples, who were brought before the council. The very men who eagerly cried for the blood of the Just One were there. They had heard Peter's cowardly denial of Jesus, with cursing and swearing, as he was accused of being one of his disciples. They thought to intimidate Peter; but he was now converted. An opportunity was here given Peter to exalt Jesus. He once denied him; but he could now remove the stain of that hasty, cowardly denial, and honor the name he had denied. No cowardly fears reigned in the breast of Peter then; but with holy boldness, and in the power of the Holy Spirit, he fearlessly declared unto them that by the name of Jesus

Christ of Nazareth, whom ye crucified, whom God raised from the dead, even by him doth this man stand here before you whole. This is the stone which was set at naught of you builders, which has become the head stone of the corner. Neither is there salvation in any other; for there is none other name under heaven given among men, whereby we must be saved.

The people were astonished at the boldness of Peter and John. They took knowledge of them that they had been with Jesus; for their noble, fearless conduct compared well with the appearance of Jesus when he was persecuted by his murderers. Jesus, by one look of pity and sorrow, reproved Peter after he had denied him, and now as he boldly acknowledged his Lord, Peter was approved and blessed. As a token of the approbation of Jesus, he was filled with the Holy Spirit.

The chief priests dared not manifest the hate they felt towards the disciples. They commanded them to go aside out of the council, and they conferred among themselves, saying, What shall we do to these men? for that indeed a notable miracle hath been done by them is manifest to all them that dwell in Jerusalem, and we cannot deny it. They were afraid to have this good work spread. If it should spread, their power would be lost, and they would be looked upon as the murderers of Jesus. All that they dared to do was to threaten them, and command them to speak no more in the name of Jesus lest they die. But Peter declared boldly that they could but speak the things which they had seen and heard.

By the power of Jesus the disciples continued to heal every one of the afflicted and the sick which were brought to them. The high priests and elders, and those particularly engaged with them, were alarmed. Hundreds were enlisting daily under the banner of a crucified, risen and ascended Saviour. They shut the apostles up in prison, and hoped that the excitement would subside. Satan triumphed, and the evil angels exulted; but the angels of God were sent and opened the prison doors, and, contrary to the command of the high priest and elders, bade them go into the temple, and speak all the words of this life. The council assembled and sent for their prisoners. The officers unclosed the prison doors; but the prisoners whom they sought were not there. They returned to the priests and elders, and said to them, The prison truly found we shut with all safety, and the keepers standing without before the doors; but when we had opened we found no man within. Then came one and told them, saying, Behold the men whom ye put in prison are standing in the temple, and teaching the people. Then went the captain with the officers, and brought them without violence; for they feared the people lest they should have been stoned. And when they had brought them, they set them before the council; and the high priest asked them, Did not we straitly command you, that ye should not teach in this name? and, behold, ye have filled Jerusalem with your doctrine, and intend to bring this man's blood upon us.

They were hypocrites, and loved the praise of men more than they loved God. Their hearts were hardened, and the most mighty acts wrought by the apostles only enraged them. They knew that if the disciples preached Jesus, his crucifixion, resurrection and ascension, it would fasten guilt upon them, and proclaim them his murderers. They were not as willing to receive the blood of Jesus as when they vehemently cried, His blood be on us, and on our children.

The apostles boldly declared that they ought to obey God rather than man. Said Peter, The God of our fathers raised up Jesus, whom ye slew and hanged on a tree. Him hath God exalted with his right hand to be a Prince and a Saviour, for to give repentance to Israel, and forgiveness of sins. And we are his witnesses of these things, and so is also the Holy Spirit whom God hath given to them that obey him. Then were those murderers enraged. They wished to imbrue their hands in blood again by slaying the apostles. They were planning how to do this, when an angel from God was sent to Gamaliel to move upon his heart to counsel the chief priest and rulers. Said Gamaliel, Refrain from these men, and let them alone; for if this counsel or this work be of men, it will come to naught; but if it be of God ye cannot overthrow it; lest haply ye be found even to fight against God. The evil angels were moving upon the priests and elders to put the apostles to death; but God sent his angel to prevent it, by raising up a voice in favor of the disciples in their own ranks.

The work of the apostles was not finished. They were to be brought before kings, to witness to the name of Jesus, and to testify to the things which they had seen and heard. But before these chief priests and elders let them go, they beat them, and commanded them to speak no more in the name of Jesus. They departed from the council praising God that they were accounted worthy to suffer for his dear name. They continued their mission, preaching in the temple and in every house where they were invited. The word of God grew and multiplied. Satan had moved upon the chief priests and elders to hire the Roman guard to falsely say that the disciples stole Jesus while they slept. Through this lie they hoped to conceal the facts; but, lo, springing up all around them were the mighty evidences of Jesus' resurrection. The disciples boldly declared it, and testified to the things which they had seen and heard, and through the name of Jesus they performed mighty miracles. They boldly placed the blood of Jesus upon those who were so willing to receive it, when they were permitted to have power over the Son of God.

I saw that the angels of God were commissioned to have a special care, and guard the sacred, important truths which were to serve as an anchor to hold the disciples of Christ through every generation.

The Holy Spirit especially rested upon the apostles, who were witnesses of Jesus' crucifixion, resurrection and ascension -- important truths which were to be the hope of Israel. All were to look to the Saviour of the world as their only hope, and walk in the way Jesus opened by the sacrifice of his own life, and keep God's law and live. I saw the wisdom and goodness of Jesus in giving power to the disciples to carry on the same work which caused the Jews to hate and slay him. They had power given them over the works of Satan. They wrought signs and wonders through the name of Jesus, who was despised, and by wicked hands slain. A halo of light and glory clustered about the time of Jesus' death and resurrection, immortalizing the sacred facts that he was the Saviour of the world.

See Acts chap.3-5

CHAPTER 13

The Death of Stephen

Disciples multiplied greatly in Jerusalem. The word of God increased, and many of the priests were obedient unto the faith. Stephen, full of faith, was doing great wonders and miracles among the people. Many were angry; for the priests were turning from their traditions, and from the sacrifices and offerings, and were accepting Jesus as the great sacrifice. Stephen, with power from on high, reproved the priests and elders, and exalted Jesus before them. They could not withstand the wisdom and power by which he spoke, and as they found that they could prevail nothing against him, they hired men to falsely swear that they had heard him speak blasphemous words against Moses and against God. They stirred up the people, and took Stephen, and, through false witnesses, accused him of speaking against the temple and the law. They testified that they had heard him say that this Jesus of Nazareth would destroy the customs which Moses gave them.

All who sat in judgment against Stephen saw the light of the glory of God in his countenance. His countenance was lighted up like the face of an angel. He stood up full of faith and the Holy Spirit, and, beginning at the prophets, he brought them down to the advent of Jesus, his crucifixion, his resurrection and ascension, and showed them that the Lord dwelt not in temples made with hands. They worshiped the temple. Anything spoken against the temple filled them with greater indignation than if spoken against God. The spirit of Stephen was stirred with heavenly indignation as he cried out against them for being wicked, and uncircumcised in heart. Ye do always resist the Holy Spirit. They observed the outward ordinances, while their hearts were corrupt, and full of deadly evil. Stephen referred them to the cruelty of their fathers in persecuting the prophets, saying, Ye have slain them which showed before the coming of the Just One, of whom ye have been now the betrayers and murderers.

The chief priests and the rulers were enraged as the plain, cutting truths were spoken; and they rushed upon Stephen. The light of heaven shone upon him, and as he looked up steadfastly into heaven, a vision of God's glory was given him, and angels hovered around him. He cried out, Behold, I see the heavens opened, and the Son of man standing on the right hand of God. The people would not hear him. They cried out with a loud voice, and stopped their ears, and ran upon him with one accord, and cast him out of the city, and stoned him. And Stephen kneeled down, and cried with a loud voice, Lord, lay not this sin to their charge.

I saw that Stephen was a mighty man of God, especially raised up to fill an important place in the church. Satan exulted as he was stoned to death; for he knew that the disciples would greatly feel his loss. But Satan's triumph was short; for there was one standing in that company, witnessing the death of Stephen, to whom Jesus was to reveal himself. Although he took no part in casting the stones at Stephen, yet he consented to his death. Saul was zealous in persecuting the church of God, hunting them, seizing them in their houses, and delivering them to those who would slay them. Satan was using Saul effectually. But God can break the Devil's power, and set free those who are led captive by him. Saul was a learned man, and Satan was triumphantly employing his talents to help carry out his rebellion against the Son of God, and those who believed in him. But Jesus selected Saul as a chosen vessel to preach his name, to strengthen the disciples in their work, and more than fill the place of Stephen. Saul was greatly esteemed by the Jews. His zeal and his learning pleased them, and terrified many of the disciples.

See Acts chap. 6 & 7

CHAPTER 14

The Conversion of Saul

As Saul journeyed to Damascus with letters of authority to take men or women who were preaching Jesus, and to bring them bound unto Jerusalem, evil angels exulted around him. But as he journeyed, suddenly a light from heaven shone around him, which made the evil angels flee, and caused Saul to fall quickly to the ground. He heard a voice saying, Saul, Saul, why persecutest thou me? Saul inquired, Who art thou, Lord? And the Lord said, I am Jesus whom thou persecutest. It is hard for thee to kick against the pricks. And Saul trembling and astonished said, Lord, what wilt thou have me to do? And the Lord said, Arise and go into the city, and it shall be told thee what thou must do.

The men who were with him stood speechless, hearing a voice, but saw no man. As the light passed away, and Saul arose from the earth, and opened his eyes, he saw no man. The glory of the light of heaven had blinded him. They led him by the hand, and brought him to Damascus, and he was three days without sight, neither did he eat or drink. The Lord then sent his angel to one of the very men whom Saul hoped to make captive, and revealed to him in vision that he should go into the street called straight, and inquire in the house of Judas for one called Saul of Tarsus; for, behold, he prayeth, and hath seen in a vision a man named Ananias coming in, and putting his hands on him, that he might receive his sight.

Ananias feared that there was some mistake in this matter, and began to relate to the Lord what he had heard of Saul. But the Lord said unto Ananias, Go thy way; for he is a chosen vessel unto me, to bear my name before the Gentiles, and kings, and the children of Israel. For I will show him how great things he must suffer for my name's sake. Ananias followed the directions of the Lord, and entered into the house, and putting his hands on him, said, Brother Saul, the Lord, even Jesus, that appeared unto thee in the way as thou camest, hath sent me, that thou mightest receive thy sight, and be filled with the Holy Spirit.

Immediately Saul received sight, and arose, and was baptized. He then preached Christ in the synagogues, that he was the Son of God. All who heard him were amazed, and inquired, Is not this he that destroyed them which called on this name in Jerusalem? and came hither on that intent, that he might bring them bound unto the chief priests. But Saul increased the more in strength, and confounded the Jews. They were again in trouble. Saul told his experience in the power of the Holy Spirit. All were acquainted with the fact of Saul's opposition to Jesus, and his zeal in hunting out and delivering up to death all who believed on his name. His miraculous conversion convinced many that Jesus was the Son of God. Saul related his experience, that as he was persecuting unto the death, binding and delivering into prison, both men and women, as he journeyed to Damascus, suddenly a great light from heaven shone round about him, and Jesus revealed himself to him, and taught him that he was the Son of God. As Saul boldly preached Jesus, he carried a powerful influence with him. He had knowledge of the scriptures, and after his conversion a divine light shone upon the prophecies concerning Jesus, which enabled him to clearly and boldly present the truth, and to correct any perversion of the scriptures. With the Spirit of God resting upon him, he would in a clear and forcible manner carry his hearers down through the prophecies to the time of Christ's first advent, and show them that the scriptures had been fulfilled, which referred to Christ's sufferings, death and resurrection.

See Acts chap.9

CHAPTER 15

The Jews Decided to Kill Paul

The chief priests and rulers were moved with hatred against Paul, as they witnessed the effect of the relation of his experience. They saw that he boldly preached Jesus, and wrought miracles in his name, and that multitudes listened to him, and turned from their traditions, and looked upon them as being the murderers of the Son of God. Their anger was kindled, and they assembled to consult as to what was best to be done to put down the excitement. They agreed that the only safe course for them was to put Paul to death. But God knew of their intention, and angels were commissioned to guard him, that he might live to fulfill his mission, and to suffer for the name of Jesus.

Paul was informed that the Jews were seeking his life. Satan led the unbelieving Jews to watch the gates of Damascus day and night, that as Paul should pass out of the gates; they might immediately kill him. But the disciples in the night let him down by the wall in a basket. Here the Jews were made ashamed of their failure, and Satan's object was defeated. And Paul went to Jerusalem to join himself to the disciples; but they were all afraid of him. They could not believe that he was a disciple. His life had been hunted by the Jews in Damascus, and his own brethren would not receive him; but Barnabas took him, and brought him to the apostles, and declared unto them how he had seen the Lord in the way, and that he had preached boldly at Damascus in the name of Jesus.

But Satan was stirring up the Jews to destroy Paul, and Jesus bade him leave Jerusalem. And as he went into other cities preaching Jesus, and working miracles, many were converted, and as one man was healed who had always been lame, the people who worshiped idols were about to sacrifice to the disciples. Paul was grieved, and told them that they were only men, and that they must worship God who made heaven and earth, and the sea, and all things that are therein. Paul exalted God before them; but he could scarcely restrain the people. The first knowledge of faith in the true God, and the worship and honor due to him, were being formed in their minds; and as they were listening to Paul, Satan urged on the unbelieving Jews of other cities to follow after Paul to destroy the good work wrought through him. The Jews stirred up, and inflamed the minds of those idolators by false reports against Paul. The wonder and admiration of the people now changed to hate, and they who a short time before were ready to worship the disciples, stoned Paul, and drew him out of the city, supposing that he was dead. But as the disciples were standing about Paul, and mourning over him, to their joy he rose up, and went with them into the city.

As Paul preached Jesus, a certain woman possessed with a spirit of divination, followed them, crying, These men are the servants of the most high God, which show unto us the way of salvation. Thus she followed the disciples many days. But Paul was grieved; for this crying after them diverted the minds of the people from the truth. Satan's object in leading her to do this was to disgust the people, and destroy the influence of the disciples. But Paul's spirit was stirred within him, and he turned to the woman, and said to the spirit, I command thee in the name of Jesus Christ to come out of her, and the evil spirit was rebuked, and left her.

Her masters were pleased that she cried after the disciples; but when the evil spirit had left her, and they saw her a meek disciple of Christ, they were enraged. They had gathered much money by her fortune-telling, and now the hope of their gain was gone. Satan's object was defeated; but his servants caught Paul and Silas, and drew them into the market place, unto the rulers, and to the magistrates, saying, These men being Jews do exceedingly trouble our city. And the multitude rose up together against them, and the magistrates tore off their clothes, and commanded to beat them. And when they had laid many stripes upon them, they cast them into prison, charging the jailer to keep them safely, who, having received such a charge, thrust them into the inner prison and made their feet fast in the stocks. But the angels of God accompanied them within the prison walls. Their imprisonment told to the glory of God, and showed to the people that God was in the work, and with his chosen servants, and that prison walls could be shaken, and strong iron bars could easily be opened by him.

At midnight Paul and Silas prayed, and sung praises unto God, and suddenly there was a great earthquake, so that the foundations of the prison were shaken; and I saw that immediately the angel of God loosed everyone's bands. The keeper of the prison awoke and was affrighted as he saw the prison doors open. He thought that the prisoners had escaped, and that he must be punished with death. As he was about to kill himself, Paul cried with a loud voice, saying, Do thyself no harm, for we are all here. The power of God convicted the keeper. He called for a light, and sprang in, and came trembling, and fell down before Paul and Silas, and brought them out, and said, Sirs, what must I do to be saved? And they said, Believe on the Lord Jesus Christ, and thou shalt be saved, and thy house. The jailer then assembled his whole household, and Paul preached unto them Jesus. The jailer's heart was united to those brethren, and he washed their stripes, and he, and all his house, were baptized that night. He then set meat before them, and rejoiced, believing in God, with all his house.

The wonderful news was spread abroad of the glorious power of God which had been manifest in opening the prison doors, and the conversion and baptism of the jailer and his family. The rulers heard of these things, and were afraid, and sent to the jailer, requesting him to let Paul and Silas go. But Paul would not leave the prison in a private manner. He said unto them, They have beaten us openly uncondemned, being Romans, and have cast us into prison; and now do they thrust us out privily? Nay, verily; but let them come themselves, and fetch us out. Paul and Silas were not willing that the manifestation of the power of God should be concealed. The sergeants told these words unto the magistrates; and they feared when they heard that they were Romans. And they came and besought them, and brought them out, and desired them to depart out of the city.

See Acts chap.14&16

CHAPTER 16

Paul Visited Jerusalem

Shortly after Paul's conversion he visited Jerusalem, and preached Jesus, and the wonder of his grace. He related his miraculous conversion, which enraged the priests, and rulers, and they sought to take his life. But that his life might be saved, Jesus appeared to him again in a vision while he was praying, saying unto him, Get thee quickly out of Jerusalem; for they will not receive thy testimony concerning me. Paul earnestly plead with Jesus, Lord, they know that I imprisoned and beat in every synagogue them that believed on thee. And when the blood of thy martyr Stephen was shed, I also was standing by and consenting unto his death, and kept the raiment of them that slew him. Paul thought the Jews in Jerusalem could not resist his testimony; that they would consider that the great change in him could only be wrought by the power of God. But Jesus said unto him, Depart, for I will send thee far hence unto the Gentiles.

In Paul's absence from Jerusalem, he wrote many letters to different places, relating his experience, and bearing a powerful testimony. But some strove to destroy the influence of those letters. They had to admit that his letters were weighty and powerful; but declared that his bodily presence was weak, and his speech contemptible.

I saw that Paul was a man of great learning, and his wisdom and manners charmed his hearers. Learned men were pleased with his knowledge, and many of them believed on Jesus. When before kings and large assemblies, he would pour forth such eloquence as would bear down all before him. This greatly enraged the priests and elders. Paul could readily enter into deep reasoning, and soar up, and carry the people with him, in the most exalted trains of thought, and bring to view the deep riches of the grace of God, and portray before them the amazing love of Christ. Then with simplicity he would come down to the understanding of the common people, and in a most powerful manner relate his experience, which called forth from them ardent desires to be the disciples of Christ.

The Lord revealed to Paul that he must again go up to Jerusalem; that he would there be bound and suffer for his name. And although he was a prisoner for a great length of time, yet the Lord was carrying forward his special work through him. Paul's bonds were to be the means of spreading the knowledge of Christ, and thus glorifying God. As he was sent from city to city for his trial, the testimony concerning Jesus, and the interesting incidents of his conversion were related before kings and governors, that they should not be left without testimony concerning Jesus. Thousands believed on him and rejoiced in his name. I saw that God's special purpose was fulfilled in the journey of Paul upon the water, that the ship's crew might witness the power of God through Paul, and that the heathen also might hear the name of Jesus, and many be converted through his teaching, and by witnessing the miracles he wrought. Kings and governors were charmed by his reasoning, and as, with zeal and the power of the Holy Spirit, he preached Jesus, and related the interesting events of his experience, conviction fastened upon them that Jesus was the Son of God; and while some wondered with amazement as they listened to Paul, one cried out, Almost thou persuadest me to be a Christian. Yet they thought that at some future time they would consider what they had heard. Satan took advantage of the delay, and as they neglected that opportunity when their hearts were softened, it was forever. Their hearts became hardened.

I was shown the work of Satan in first blinding the eyes of the Jews so that they would not receive Jesus as their Saviour; and next in leading them, through envy because of his mighty works, to desire his life. Satan entered one of Jesus' own followers, and led him on to betray him into their hands, and they crucified the Lord of life and glory. After Jesus arose from the dead, the Jews added sin to sin as they sought to hide the fact of the resurrection, by hiring for money the Roman guard to testify to a falsehood. But the resurrection of Jesus was made doubly sure by the resurrection of a multitude of witnesses who arose with him. Jesus appeared to his disciples, and to above five hundred at once, while those whom he brought up with him appeared unto many declaring that Jesus had risen.

Satan had caused the Jews to rebel against God, by refusing to receive his Son, and in staining their hands with most precious blood in crucifying him. No matter how powerful the evidence given of Jesus' being the Son of God, the Redeemer of the world; they had murdered him, and could not receive any evidence in his favor. Their only hope and consolation, like Satan's after his fall, was in trying to prevail against the Son of God. They continued their rebellion by persecuting the disciples of Christ, and putting them to death. Nothing fell so harshly on their ears as the name of Jesus whom they had crucified; and they were determined not to listen to any evidence in his favor. As in the case of Stephen, as the Holy Spirit through him declared the mighty evidence of his being the Son of God, they stopped their ears lest they should be convinced. And while Stephen was wrapped up in God's glory, they stoned him to death. Satan had the murderers of Jesus fast in his grasp. By wicked works they had yielded themselves his willing subjects, and through them he was at work to trouble and annoy the believers of Christ. He worked through the Jews to stir up the Gentiles against the name of Jesus, and against those who followed him, and believed on his name. But God sent his angels to strengthen the disciples for their work, that they might testify of the things they had seen and heard, and at last in their steadfastness, seal their testimony with their blood.

Satan rejoiced that the Jews were safe in his snare. They still continued their useless forms, their sacrifices and ordinances. As Jesus hung upon the cross, and cried, *It is finished*, the vail of the temple was rent in twain, from the top to the bottom, to signify that God would no longer meet with the priests in the temple, to accept their sacrifices and ordinances; and also to show that the partition wall was broken down between the Jews and the Gentiles. Jesus had made an offering of himself for both, and if saved at all, both must believe in Jesus as the only offering for sin, and the Saviour of the world.

While Jesus hung upon the cross, as the soldier pierced his side with a spear, there came out blood and water, in two distinct streams, one of blood, the other of clear water. The blood was to wash away the sins of those who should believe in his name. The water represents that living water which is obtained from Jesus to give life to the believer.

See Matthew 27:51; John 19:34; Acts chap. 24 & 26

CHAPTER 17

The Great Apostasy

I was carried forward to the time when the heathen idolators cruelly persecuted the Christians, and killed them. Blood flowed in torrents. The noble, the learned, and the common people, were alike slain without mercy. Wealthy families were reduced to poverty because they would not yield their religion. Notwithstanding the persecution and sufferings those Christians endured, they would not lower the standard. They kept their religion pure. I saw that Satan exulted and triumphed over the sufferings of God's people. But God looked with great approbation upon his faithful martyrs, and the Christians who lived in that fearful time were greatly beloved of him; for they were willing to suffer for his sake. Every suffering endured by them increased their reward in heaven. But although Satan rejoiced because the saints suffered, yet he was not satisfied. He wanted control of the mind as well as the body. The sufferings those Christians endured drove them closer to the Lord, and led them to love one another, and caused them to fear more than ever to offend him. Satan wished to lead them to displease God; then they would lose their strength, fortitude and firmness. Although thousands were slain, yet others were springing up to supply their place. Satan saw that he was losing his subjects, and although they suffered persecution and death, yet they were secured to Jesus Christ, to be the subjects of his kingdom, and he laid his plans to more successfully fight against the government of God, and overthrow the church. He led on those heathen idolators to embrace part of the Christian faith. They professed to believe in the crucifixion and resurrection of Christ, without a change of heart, and proposed to unite with the followers of Jesus. O the fearful danger of the church! It was a time of mental anguish. Some thought that if they should come down and unite with those idolators who had embraced a portion of the Christian faith, it would be the means of their conversion. Satan was seeking to corrupt the doctrines of the Bible. At last I saw the standard lowered, and the heathen were uniting with Christians. They had been worshipers of idols, and although they professed to be Christians, they brought along with them their idolatry. They changed the objects only of their worship, to images of saints, and even the image of Christ, and Mary the mother of Jesus. Christians gradually united with them, and the Christian religion was corrupted, and the church lost its purity and power. Some refused to unite with them and they preserved their purity, and worshiped God alone. They would not bow down to any image of anything in the heavens above, or in the earth beneath.

Satan exulted over the fall of so many; and then he stirred up the fallen church to force those who would preserve the purity of their religion, to either yield to their ceremonies and image worship, or to put them to death. The fires of persecution were again kindled against the true church of Jesus Christ, and millions were slain without mercy.

It was presented before me in the following manner: A large company of heathen idolators bore a black banner upon which were figures of the sun, moon and stars. The company seemed to be very fierce and angry. I was then shown another company bearing a pure white banner, and upon it was written Purity, and Holiness unto the Lord. Their countenances were marked with firmness and heavenly resignation. I saw the heathen idolators approach them, and there was a great slaughter. The Christians melted away before them; and yet the Christian company pressed the more closely together, and held the banner more firmly. As many fell, others rallied around the banner and filled their places.

I saw the company of idolators consulting together. They failed to make the Christians yield, and they agreed to another plan. I saw them lower their banner, and they approached that firm Christian company, and made propositions to them. At first their propositions were utterly refused. Then I saw the Christian company consulting together. Some said that they would lower the banner, accept the propositions, and save their lives, and at last they could gain strength to raise their banner among those heathen idolators. But some would not yield to this plan, but firmly chose to die holding their banner, rather than lower it. Then I saw many of that Christian company lower the banner, and unite with the heathen; while the firm and steadfast seized the banner, and bore it high again. I saw individuals continually leaving the company of those bearing the pure banner, and joining the idolators, and they united together under the black banner, to persecute those bearing the white banner, and many were slain; yet the white banner was held high, and individuals were raised up to rally around it.

The Jews who first started the rage of the heathen against Jesus, were not to escape. In the judgment hall the infuriated Jews cried, as Pilate hesitated to condemn Jesus, His blood be on us and on our children. The race of the Jews experienced the fulfillment of this terrible curse which they called down upon their own heads. Heathen and those called Christians were alike their foes. Those professed Christians, in their zeal for the cross of Christ, because the Jews had crucified Jesus, thought that the more suffering they could bring upon them, the better could they please God; and many of those unbelieving Jews were killed, while others were driven from place to place, and were punished in almost every manner.

The blood of Christ, and of the disciples, whom they had put to death, was upon them, and in terrible judgments were they visited. The curse of God followed them, and they were a by-word and a derision to the heathen and to Christians. They were shunned, degraded and detested, as though the brand of Cain was upon them. Yet I saw that God marvelously preserved this people, and had scattered them over the world, that they might be looked upon as especially visited by a curse from God. I saw that God had forsaken the Jews as a nation; yet there was a portion of them who would be enabled to tear the veil from their hearts. Some will yet see that prophecy has been fulfilled concerning them, and they will receive Jesus as the Saviour of the world, and see the great sin of their nation in rejecting Jesus, and crucifying him. Individuals among the Jews will be converted; but as a nation they are forever forsaken of God.

CHAPTER 18

Mystery of Iniquity

It has ever been the design of Satan to draw the minds of the people from Jesus to man, and to destroy individual accountability. Satan failed in his design when he tempted the Son of God. He succeeded better as he came to fallen man. The doctrine of Christianity was corrupted. Popes and priests presumed to take an exalted position, and taught the people to look to them to pardon their sins, instead of looking to Christ for themselves. The Bible was kept from them, in order to conceal the truths which would condemn them.

The people were entirely deceived. They were taught that the popes and priests were Christ's representatives, when in fact they were the representatives of Satan; and when they bowed to them, they worshiped Satan. The people called for the Bible; but the priests considered it dangerous to let them have the word of God to read for themselves, lest they become enlightened, and their sins be exposed. The people were taught to look to these deceivers, and receive every word from them, as from the mouth of God. They held that power over the mind, which God alone should hold. And if any dared to follow their own convictions, the same hate which Satan and the Jews exercised towards Jesus would be kindled against them, and those in authority would thirst for their blood. I was shown a time when Satan especially triumphed. Multitudes of Christians were slain in a dreadful manner because they would preserve the purity of their religion.

The Bible was hated, and efforts were made to rid the earth of the precious word of God. The Bible was forbidden to be read on pain of death, and all the copies of the holy Book which could be found were burned. But I saw that God had a special care for his word. He protected it. At different periods there were but a very few copies of the Bible in existence, yet God would not suffer his word to be lost. And in the last days, copies of the Bible were to be so multiplied that every family could possess it. I saw that when there were but a very few copies of the Bible, it was precious and comforting to the persecuted followers of Jesus. It was read in the most secret manner, and those who had this exalted privilege felt that they had had an interview with God, with his Son Jesus, and with his disciples. But this blessed privilege cost many of them their lives. If discovered, they were taken from reading the sacred Word to the chopping block, the stake, or to the dungeon to die from starvation.

Satan could not hinder the plan of salvation. Jesus was crucified, and arose again the third day. He told his angels that he would make even the crucifixion and resurrection tell to his advantage. He was willing that those who professed faith in Jesus should believe that the laws regulating the Jewish sacrifices and offerings ceased at the death of Christ, if he could push them further, and make them believe that the law of ten commandments died also with Christ.

I saw that many readily yielded to this device of Satan. All heaven was moved with indignation, as they saw the holy law of God trampled under foot. Jesus and all the heavenly host were acquainted with the nature of God's law; they knew that he would not change or abolish it. The hopeless condition of man caused the deepest sorrow in heaven, and moved Jesus to offer to die for the transgressors of God's holy law. If his law could be abolished, man might have been saved without the death of Jesus. The death of Christ did not destroy the law of his Father; but magnified and honored it, and enforces obedience to all its holy precepts. Had the church remained pure and steadfast, Satan could not have deceived them, and led them to trample on the law of God. In this bold plan, Satan strikes directly against the foundation of God's government in heaven and on earth. His rebellion caused him to be expelled from heaven. After he rebelled, in order to save himself, he wished God to change his law; but God told Satan, before the whole heavenly host, that his law was unalterable. Satan knows that if he can cause others to violate God's law he is sure of them; for every transgressor of his law must die.

Satan decided to go still further. He told his angels that some would be so jealous of God's law that they could not be caught in this snare; that the ten commandments were so plain that many would believe that they were still binding; therefore he must seek to corrupt the fourth commandment which brings to view the living God. He led on his representatives to attempt to change the Sabbath, and alter the only commandment of the ten which brings to view the true God, the maker of the heavens and the earth. Satan presented before them the glorious resurrection of Jesus, and told them that by his rising on the first day of the week, he changed the Sabbath from the seventh to the first day of the week. Thus Satan used the resurrection to serve his purpose. He and his angels rejoiced that the errors they had prepared took so well with the professed friends of Christ. What one might look upon with religious horror, another would receive. The different errors would be received, and with zeal defended. The will of God plainly revealed in his word, was covered up with error and tradition, which have been taught as the commandments of God. But although this heaven-daring deception was to be suffered to be carried on down through time until the second appearing of Jesus, yet through all this time of error and deception, God has not been left without a witness. There have been true and faithful witnesses keeping all of God's commandments through the darkness and persecution of the church.

I saw that angels were filled with amazement as they beheld the sufferings and death of the King of glory. But I saw that it was no marvel to the angelic host that the Lord of life and glory, who filled all heaven with joy and splendor, should break the bands of death, and walk forth from his prison house a triumphant conqueror. And if either of these events should be commemorated by a day of rest, it is the crucifixion. But, I saw that neither of those events were designed to alter or abolish God's law; but they give the strongest proof of its immutability.

Both of these important events have their memorials. By partaking of the Lord's supper, the broken bread and the fruit of the vine, we show forth the Lord's death until he comes. By observing this memorial, the scenes of his sufferings and death are brought fresh to our minds. The resurrection of Christ is commemorated by our being buried with him by baptism, and raised up out of the watery grave in likeness of his resurrection, to live in newness of life.

I was shown that the law of God would stand fast forever, and exist in the new earth to all eternity. At the creation, when the foundations of the earth were laid, the sons of God looked with admiration upon the work of the Creator, and all the heavenly host shouted for joy. It was then that the foundation of the Sabbath was laid. At the close of the six days of creation, God rested on the seventh day from all his work which he had made; and he blessed the seventh day and sanctified it, because that in it he had rested from all his work. The Sabbath was instituted in Eden before the fall, and was observed by Adam and Eve, and all the heavenly host. God rested on the seventh day, and blessed and hallowed it; and I saw that the Sabbath would never be done away; but the redeemed saints, and all the angelic host, will observe it in honor of the great Creator to all eternity.

See Daniel chap. 7; 2 Thessalonians chap. 2

CHAPTER 19

Death, Not Eternal Life in Misery

Satan commenced his deception in Eden. He said to Eve, Thou shalt not surely die. This was Satan's first lesson upon the immortality of the soul; and he has carried on this deception from that time to the present, and will carry it on until the captivity of God's children shall be turned. I was pointed to Adam and Eve in Eden. They partook of the forbidden tree, and then the flaming sword was placed around the tree of life, and they were driven from the Garden, lest they should partake of the tree of life, and be immortal sinners. The tree of life was to perpetuate immortality. I heard an angel ask, Who of the family of Adam have passed that flaming sword, and have partaken of the tree of life? I heard another angel answer, Not one of the family of Adam have passed that flaming sword, and partaken of that tree; therefore there is not an immortal sinner. The soul that sinneth it shall die an everlasting death; a death that will last forever, where there will be no hope of a resurrection; and then the wrath of God will be appeased.

It was a marvel to me that Satan could succeed so well in making men believe that the words of God, The soul that sinneth it shall die, mean that the soul that sinneth it shall not die, but live eternally in misery. Said the angel, Life is life, whether it is in pain or happiness. Death is without pain, without joy, without hatred.

Satan told his angels to make a special effort to spread the deception and lie first repeated to Eve in Eden, Thou shalt not surely die. And as the error was received by the people, and they believed that man was immortal, Satan led them still further to believe that the sinner would live in eternal misery. Then the way was prepared for Satan to work through his representatives, and hold up God before the people as a revengeful tyrant; that those who do not please him, he will plunge into hell, and cause them ever to feel his wrath; and that they will suffer unutterable anguish, while he will look down upon them with satisfaction, as they writhe in horrible sufferings and eternal flames. Satan knew that if this error should be received, God would be dreaded and hated by very many, instead of being loved and admired; and that many would be led to believe that the threatenings of God's word would not be literally fulfilled; for it would be against his character of benevolence and love, to plunge beings whom he had created into eternal torments. Satan has led them to another extreme, to entirely overlook the justice of God, and the threatenings in his Word, and represent him as being all mercy, and that not one will perish, but all, both saint and sinner, will at last be saved in his kingdom. In consequence of the popular error of the immortality of the soul, and endless misery, Satan takes advantage of another class, and leads them on to regard the Bible as an uninspired book. They think it teaches many good things; but they cannot rely upon it and love it; because they have been taught that it declares the doctrine of eternal misery.

Satan takes advantage of still another class, and leads them still further to deny the existence of God. They can see no consistency in the character of the God of the Bible, if he will torment a portion of the human family to all eternity in horrible tortures; and they deny the Bible and its Author, and regard death as an eternal sleep.

Then Satan leads another class who are fearful and timid to commit sin; and after they have sinned, he holds up before them that the wages of sin is not death, but an eternal life in horrible torments, to be endured through the endless ages of eternity. Satan improves the opportunity, and magnifies before their feeble minds the horrors of an endless hell, and takes charge of their minds, and they lose their reason. Then Satan and his angels exult, and the infidel and atheist join in casting reproach upon Christianity. They regard these evil consequences of the reception of popular heresy, as the natural results of believing in the Bible and its Author.

I saw that the heavenly host was filled with indignation at this bold work of Satan. I inquired why all these delusions should be suffered to take effect upon the minds of men, when the angels of God were powerful, and if commissioned, could easily break the enemy's power. Then I saw that God knew that Satan would try every art to destroy man; therefore he had caused his Word to be written out, and had made his designs to man so plain that the weakest need not err. Then, after he had given his Word to man, he had carefully preserved it, so that Satan and his angels, through any agent or representative, could not destroy it. While other books might be destroyed, this holy Book was to be immortal. And down near the close of time, when the delusions of Satan should increase, the copies of this Book were to be so multiplied, that all who desired it might have a copy of God's revealed will to man, and, if they would, might arm themselves against the deceptions and lying wonders of Satan.

I saw that God had especially guarded the Bible, yet learned men, when the copies were few, had changed the words in some instances, thinking that they were making it more plain, when they were mystifying that which was plain, in causing it to lean to their established views, governed by tradition. But I saw that the word of God, as a whole, is a perfect chain, one portion of scripture explaining another. True seekers for truth need not err; for not only is the word of God plain and simple in declaring the way to life, but the Holy Spirit is given to guide in understanding the way of life revealed in his Word.

I saw that the angels of God were never to control the will. God sets before man life and death. He can have his choice. Many desire life, but continue to walk in the broad road, because they have not chosen life.

I saw the mercy and compassion of God in giving his Son to die for guilty man. Those who will not choose to accept salvation which has been so dearly purchased for them, must be punished. Beings whom God created have chosen to rebel against his government; but I saw that God did not shut them up in hell to endure endless misery. He could not take them to heaven; for to bring them into the company of the pure and holy would make them perfectly miserable. God will not take them to heaven, neither will he cause them to suffer eternally. He will destroy them utterly, and cause them to be as though they had not been, and then his justice will be satisfied. He formed man out of the dust of the earth, and the disobedient and unholy will be consumed by fire, and return to dust again. I saw that the benevolence and compassion of God in this, should lead all to admire his character, and to adore him; and after the wicked shall be destroyed from off the earth, all the heavenly host will say, Amen!

Satan looked with great satisfaction upon those who professed the name of Christ, and were closely adhering to these delusions formed by himself. His work is to still form new delusions. His power increases, and he grows more artful. He led on his representatives, the popes and the priests, to exalt themselves, and to stir up the people to bitterly persecute those who loved God, and were not willing to yield to his delusions, introduced through them. Satan moved upon his agents to destroy Christ's devoted followers. O the sufferings and agony, which they made the precious of God to endure! Angels have kept a faithful record of it all. But Satan and his evil angels exulted, and told the angels who administered to, and strengthened those suffering saints, that they would kill them, so there would not be left a true Christian upon the earth. I saw that the church of God was then pure. There was no danger of men with corrupt hearts coming into the church of God then; for the true Christian, who dared to declare his faith, was in danger of the rack, the stake, and every torture which Satan and his evil angels could invent, and put into the mind of man.

See Genesis chap.3; Ecclesiastes 9:5, 12:7; Luke 21:33; John 3:16; 2Timothy 3:16; Revelation 20:14-15, 21:1, 22:12-19

CHAPTER 20

The Reformation

But notwithstanding all the persecution and the putting to death of the saints, yet living witnesses were raised up on every hand. The angels of God were doing the work committed to their trust. They were searching in the darkest places, and were selecting out of the darkness, men who were honest at heart. They were all buried up in error, yet God selected them as he did Saul, as chosen vessels to bear his truth, and raise their voices against the sins of his professed people. The angels of God moved upon Martin Luther, Melancthon, and others in different places, to thirst for the living testimony of the word of God. The enemy had come in like a flood, and the standard must be raised up against him. Luther was chosen to breast the storm, and stand up against the ire of a fallen church, and strengthen the few who were faithful to their holy profession. He was ever fearful of offending God. He tried through works to obtain the favor of God; but he was not satisfied until a gleam of light from heaven drove the darkness from his mind, and led him to trust, not in works, but in the merits of the blood of Christ; and to come to God for himself, not through popes nor confessors, but through Jesus Christ alone. O how precious was this knowledge to Luther! He prized this new and precious light which had dawned upon his dark understanding, and had driven away his superstition, higher than the richest earthly treasure. The word of God was new. Every thing was changed. The Book he had dreaded because he could not see beauty in it, was *life*, **LIFE** to him. It was his joy, his consolation, his blessed teacher. Nothing could induce him to leave its study. He had feared death; but as he read the word of God, all his terrors disappeared, and he admired the character of God, and loved him. He searched the word of God for himself. He feasted upon the rich treasures it contained, and then he searched it for the church. He was disgusted with the sins of those in whom he had trusted for salvation. He saw very many enshrouded in the same darkness which had covered him. He anxiously sought an opportunity to point them to the Lamb of God, who alone taketh away the sin of the world. He raised his voice against the errors and sins of the Papal church, and earnestly longed to break the chain of darkness which was confining thousands, and causing them to trust in works for salvation. He longed to be enabled to open to their minds the true riches of the grace of God, and the excellence of salvation obtained through Jesus Christ. He raised his voice zealously, and in the power of the Holy Spirit, cried against the existing sins of the leaders of the church; and as he met the storm of opposition from the priests, his courage did not fail; for he firmly relied upon the strong arm of God, and confidently trusted in him for victory. And as he pushed the battle closer and closer, the rage of the priests was kindled against him. They did not wish to be reformed. They chose to be left in ease, in wanton pleasure, in wickedness. They wished the church kept in darkness.

I saw that Luther was ardent and zealous, fearless and bold in reproving sin, and advocating the truth. He cared not for wicked men and devils. He knew that he had One with him mightier than they all. Luther possessed fire, zeal, courage and boldness, and at times might go too far; but God raised up Melancthon, who was just the opposite in character, to aid Luther, and carry on the work of reformation. Melancthon was timid, fearful, cautious, and possessed great patience. He was greatly beloved of God. His knowledge was great in the Scriptures, and his judgment and wisdom was excellent. His love for the cause of God was equal to Luther's. These hearts, the Lord knit together; they were friends which were never to be separated. Luther was a great help to Melancthon when he was in danger of being fearful and slow, and Melancthon was also a great help to Luther to keep him from moving too fast. Melancthon's far-seeing cautiousness often averted trouble which would have come upon the cause, if the work had been left alone to Luther; and the work would often have failed in being pushed forward, if it had been left to Melancthon alone. I was shown the wisdom of God in choosing these two men, of different characters to carry on the work of reformation.

I was then carried back to the days of the apostles, and saw that God chose as companions an ardent and zealous Peter, and a mild, patient, meek John. Sometimes Peter was impetuous. And the beloved disciple often checked Peter, when his zeal and ardor led him too far; but it did not reform him. But after Peter had denied his Lord, and repented, and was converted, all he needed was a mild caution from John to check his ardor and zeal. The cause of Christ would often have suffered had it been left alone to John. Peter's zeal was needed. His boldness and energy often delivered them from difficulty, and silenced their enemies. John was winning. He gained many to the cause of Christ by his patient forbearance, and deep devotedness.

God raised up men to cry against the existing sins of the Papal church, and carry forward the reformation. Satan sought to destroy these living witnesses; but God made a hedge about them. Some, for the glory of his name, were permitted to seal the testimony they had borne with their blood; but there were other powerful men, like Luther and Melancthon, who could best glorify God by living and crying aloud against the sins of popes, priests and kings. They trembled before the voice of Luther. Through those chosen men, rays of light began to scatter the darkness, and very many joyfully received the light and walked in it. And when one witness was slain, two or more were raised up to fill his place.

But Satan was not satisfied. He could only have power over the body. He could not make believers yield their faith and hope. And even in death they triumphed with a bright hope of immortality at the resurrection of the just. They had more than mortal energy. They dared not sleep for a moment. They kept the Christian armor girded about them, prepared for a conflict, not merely with spiritual foes, but with Satan in the form of men, whose constant cry was, Give up your faith, or die. Those few Christians were strong in God, and more precious in his sight than half a world bearing the name of Christ, yet cowards in his cause. While the church was persecuted, they were united and loving. They were strong in God. Sinners were not permitted to unite themselves with it; neither the deceiver nor the deceived. Those only who were willing to forsake all for Christ could be his disciples. They loved to be poor, humble and Christ-like.

See Luke 22:61-62; John 18:10; Acts chap. 3 & 4

For further study see "*The Reformation*" in an encyclopedia.

CHAPTER 21

The Church and World United

Satan then consulted with his angels, and they there considered what they had gained. It was true that they had kept some timid souls through fear of death, from embracing the truth; but many, even of the most timid, received the truth, and immediately their fears and timidity left them, and as they witnessed the death of their brethren, and saw their firmness and patience, they knew that God and angels assisted them to endure such sufferings, and they grew bold and fearless. And when called to yield their own lives, they maintained their faith with such patience and firmness as caused even their murderers to tremble. Satan and his angels decided that there was a more successful way to destroy souls, and more certain in the end. They saw that although they caused Christians to suffer, their steadfastness, and the bright hope that cheered them, caused the weakest to grow strong, and that the rack and the flames could not daunt them. They imitated the noble bearing of Christ when before his murderers, and many were convinced of the truth by witnessing their constancy, and the glory of God which rested upon them. Satan decided that he must come in a milder form. He had corrupted the doctrines of the Bible; and traditions which were to ruin millions were taking deep root. He restrained his hate, and decided not to urge on his subjects to such bitter persecution; but lead on the church to contend, not for the faith once delivered to the saints, but, for various traditions. As he led on the church to receive favors and honors of the world, under the false pretense of benefiting them, she began to lose favor with God. Gradually the church lost her power, as she shunned to declare the straight truths which shut out the lovers of pleasure and friends of the world.

The church is not the separate and peculiar people she was when the fires of persecution were kindled against her. How is the gold become dim? How is the most fine gold changed? I saw that if the church had always retained her holy and peculiar character, the power of the Holy Spirit which was imparted to the disciples would be with her. The sick would be healed, devils would be rebuked and cast out, and she would be mighty, and a terror to her enemies.

I saw that a very large company professed the name of Christ, but God does not recognize them as his. He has no pleasure in them. Satan seemed to assume a religious character, and was very willing that the people should think they were Christians. He was very willing that they should believe in Jesus, his crucifixion, and his resurrection. Satan and his angels fully believed all this themselves, and trembled. But if this faith does not provoke to good works, and lead those who profess it to imitate the self-denying life of Christ, he is not disturbed; for they merely assume the Christian name, while their hearts are still carnal; and he can use them in his service better than if they made no profession. Under the name of Christian they hide their deformity. They pass along with their unsanctified natures, and their evil passions unsubdued. This gives occasion for the unbeliever to throw their imperfections in the face of Jesus Christ, to reproach him, and to cause those who do possess pure and undefiled religion to be brought into disrepute.

The ministers preach smooth things to suit carnal professors. This is just as Satan would have it. They dare not preach Jesus and the cutting truths of the Bible; for if they should, these carnal professors would not hear them. Many of them are wealthy and must be retained in the church, although they are no more fit to be there than Satan and his angels. The religion of Jesus is made to appear popular and honorable in the eyes of the world. The people are told that those who profess religion will be more honored by the world. Very widely do such teachings differ from the teachings of Christ. His doctrine and the world could not be at peace. Those who followed him had to renounce the world. These smooth things originated with Satan and his angels. They formed the plan, and nominal professors have carried it out. Hypocrites and sinners unite with the church. Pleasing fables are taught, and readily received. But if the truth should be preached in its purity, it would soon shut out hypocrites and sinners. But there is no difference between the professed followers of Christ and the world. I saw that if the false covering could be torn off from the members of the churches, there would be revealed such iniquity, vileness and corruption, that the most diffident child of God would have no hesitancy in calling them by their right name, children of their father, the Devil; for his works they do. Jesus and all the heavenly host looked with disgust upon the scene; yet God had a message for the church that was sacred and important. If received, it would make a thorough reformation in the church, revive the living testimony that would purge out hypocrites and sinners, and bring the church again into favor with God.

See Isaiah 30:8-21; James 2:19; Revelation chap.3

CHAPTER 22

William Miller

I saw that God sent his angel to move upon the heart of a farmer who had not believed the Bible, and led him to search the prophecies. Angels of God repeatedly visited that chosen one, and guided his mind, and opened his understanding to prophecies which had ever been dark to God's people. The commencement of the chain of truth was given to him, and he was led on to search for link after link, until he looked with wonder and admiration upon the word of God. He saw there a perfect chain of truth. That Word which he had regarded as uninspired, now opened before his vision with beauty and glory. He saw that one portion of scripture explained another, and when one portion was closed to his understanding, he found in another portion of the Word that which explained it. He regarded the sacred word of God with joy, and with the deepest respect and awe.

As he followed down the prophecies, he saw that the inhabitants of earth were living in the closing scenes of this world's history, and they knew it not. He looked at the corruptions of the churches, and saw that their love was taken from Jesus, and placed on the world, and that they were seeking for worldly honor instead of that honor which cometh from above; ambitious for worldly riches, instead of laying up their treasure in heaven. Hypocrisy, darkness and death he could see everywhere. His spirit was stirred within him. God called him to leave his farm, as Elisha was called to leave his oxen and the field of his labor to follow Elijah. With trembling, William Miller began to unfold the mysteries of the kingdom of God to the people. He gained strength with every effort. He carried the people down through the prophecies to the second advent of Christ. As John the Baptist heralded the first advent of Jesus, and prepared the way for his coming, so also, Wm. Miller and those who joined with him, proclaimed the second advent of the Son of God.

I was carried back to the days of the disciples, and was shown the beloved John, that God had a special work for him to accomplish. Satan was determined to hinder this work, and he led on his servants to destroy John. But God sent his angel and wonderfully preserved him. All who witnessed the great power of God manifested in the deliverance of John, were astonished, and many were convinced that God was with him, and that the testimony which he bore concerning Jesus was correct. Those who sought to destroy him were afraid to again attempt to take his life, and he was permitted to suffer on for Jesus. He was falsely accused by his enemies, and was shortly banished to a lonely island, where the Lord sent his angel to reveal to him things which were to take place upon the earth, and the state of the church down through to the end; her backslidings, and the position the church should occupy if she would please God, and finally overcome. The angel from heaven came to John in majesty. His countenance beamed with the excellent glory of heaven. He revealed to John scenes of deep and thrilling interest concerning the church of God, and brought before him the perilous conflicts they were to endure. John saw them pass through fiery trials, and made white and tried, and, finally, victorious overcomers, gloriously saved in the kingdom of God. The countenance of the angel grew radiant with joy, and was exceeding glorious, as he showed to John the final triumph of the church of God. John was enraptured as he beheld the final deliverance of the church, and as he was carried away with the glory of the scene, with deep reverence and awe he fell at the feet of the angel to worship him. The angel instantly raised him up, and gently reproved him, saying, See thou do it not; I am thy fellow-servant, and of thy brethren that have the testimony of Jesus; worship God; for the testimony of Jesus is the spirit of prophecy. The angel then showed John the heavenly city with all its splendor and dazzling glory. John was enraptured and overwhelmed with the glory of the city. He did not bear in mind his former reproof from the angel, but again fell to worship before the feet of the angel, who again gave the gentle reproof, See thou do it not; for I am thy fellow-servant, and of thy brethren the prophets, and of them that keep the sayings of this book; worship God.

Preachers and people have looked upon the book of Revelation as mysterious, and of less importance than other portions of the sacred Scriptures. But I saw that this book is indeed a revelation given for the especial benefit of those who should live in the last days, to guide them in ascertaining their true position, and their duty. God led the mind of Wm. Miller into the prophecies, and gave him great light upon the book of Revelation.

If Daniel's visions had been understood, the people could better have understood the visions of John. But at the right time, God moved upon his chosen servant, who with clearness and in the power of the Holy Spirit, opened the prophecies, and showed the harmony of the visions of Daniel and John, and other portions of the Bible, and pressed home upon the hearts of the people the sacred, fearful warnings of the Word, to prepare for the coming of the Son of man. Deep and solemn convictions rested upon the minds of those who heard him, and ministers and people, sinners and infidels, turned to the Lord, to seek a preparation to stand in the judgment.

Angels of God accompanied Wm. Miller in his mission. He was firm and undaunted. He fearlessly proclaimed the message committed to his trust. A world lying in wickedness, and a cold, worldly church were enough to call into action his energy, and lead him to willingly endure toil, privation and suffering. Although opposed by professed Christians and the world, and buffeted by Satan and his angels, he ceased not to preach the everlasting gospel to crowds wherever he was invited, and sound the cry, Fear God and give glory to him; for the hour of his judgment is come.

See 1 Kings 19:16-21; Daniel chap. 7-12; Revelation chap. 1, 14:7, 19:8-10, 22:6-10

CHAPTER 23

The First Angel's Message

I saw that God was in the proclamation of the time in 1843. It was his design to arouse the people, and bring them to a testing point where they should decide. Ministers were convicted and convinced of the correctness of the positions taken on the prophetic periods, and they left their pride, their salaries, and their churches, to go forth from place to place and proclaim the message. But as the message from heaven could find a place in the hearts of but a very few of the professed ministers of Christ, the work was laid upon many who were not preachers. Some left their fields to sound the message, while others were called from their shops and their merchandise. And even some professional men were compelled to leave their professions to engage in the unpopular work of giving the first angel's message. Ministers laid aside their sectarian views and feelings, and united in proclaiming the coming of Jesus. The people were moved everywhere the message reached them. Sinners repented, wept and prayed for forgiveness, and those whose lives had been marked with dishonesty, were anxious to make restitution.

Parents felt the deepest solicitude for their children. Those who received the message, labored with their unconverted friends and relatives, and with their souls bowed with the weight of the solemn message, warned and entreated them to prepare for the coming of the Son of man. Those cases were the most hardened that would not yield to such a weight of evidence set home by heart-felt warnings. This soul-purifying work led the affections away from worldly things, to a consecration never before experienced. Thousands were led to embrace the truth preached by Wm. Miller, and servants of God were raised up in the spirit and power of Elijah to proclaim the message. Those who preached this solemn message, like John the forerunner of Jesus, felt compelled to lay the axe at the root of the tree, and call upon men to bring forth fruits meet for repentance. Their testimony was calculated to arouse and powerfully affect the churches, and manifest their real character. And as they raised the solemn warning to flee from the wrath to come, many who were united with the churches received the healing message; they saw their backslidings, and, with bitter tears of repentance, and deep agony of soul, humbled themselves before God. And as the Spirit of God rested upon them, they helped to sound the cry, Fear God, and give glory to him, for the hour of his judgment is come.

The preaching of definite time called forth great opposition from all classes, from the minister in the pulpit, down to the most reckless, heaven-daring sinner. No man knoweth the day and the hour, was heard from the hypocritical minister and the bold scoffer. Neither would be instructed and corrected on the use made of the text by those who were pointing to the year when they believed the prophetic periods would run out, and to the signs which showed Christ near, even at the doors. Many shepherds of the flock, who professed to love Jesus, said they had no opposition to the preaching of Christ's coming; but they objected to the definite time. God's all-seeing eye read their hearts. They did not love Jesus near. They knew that their unchristian lives would not stand the test; for they were not walking in the humble path laid out by him. These false shepherds stood in the way of the work of God. The truth spoken in its convincing power to the people aroused them, and like the jailer, they began to inquire, What must I do to be saved. But these shepherds stepped between the truth and the people, and preached smooth things to lead them from the truth. They united with Satan and his angels, and cried, Peace, peace, when there was no peace. I saw that angels of God had marked it all, and the garments of those unconsecrated shepherds were covered with the blood of souls. Those who loved their ease, and were content with their distance from God, would not be aroused from their carnal security.

Many ministers would not accept this saving message themselves, and those who would receive it, they hindered. The blood of souls is upon them. Preachers and people joined to oppose this message from heaven. They persecuted Wm. Miller, and those who united with him in the work. Falsehoods were circulated to injure his influence, and at different times after he had plainly declared the counsel of God, applying cutting truths to the hearts of his hearers, great rage was kindled against him, and as he left the place of meeting, some waylaid him in order to take his life. But angels of God were sent to preserve his life, and they led him safely away from the angry mob. His work was not yet finished.

The most devoted gladly received the message. They knew it was from God, and that it was delivered at the right time. Angels were watching with the deepest interest the result of the heavenly message, and when the churches turned from and rejected it, they in sadness consulted with Jesus. He turned his face from the churches, and bid his angels to faithfully watch over the precious ones who did not reject the testimony, for another light was yet to shine upon them.

I saw that if professed Christians had loved their Saviour's appearing, if their affections were placed on him, if they felt that there was none upon earth to be compared with him, they would have hailed with joy the first intimation of his coming. But the dislike they manifested, as they heard of their Lord's coming, was a decided proof that they did not love him. Satan and his angels triumphed, and cast it in the face of Jesus Christ and his holy angels, that his professed people had so little love for Jesus that they did not desire his second appearing.

I saw the people of God, joyful in expectation, looking for their Lord. But God designed to prove them. His hand covered a mistake in the reckoning of the prophetic periods. Those who were looking for their Lord did not discover it, and the most learned men who opposed the time also failed to see the mistake. God designed that his people should meet with a disappointment. The time passed, and those who had looked with joyful expectation for their Saviour were sad and disheartened, while those who had not loved the appearing of Jesus, but embraced the message through fear, were pleased that he did not come at the time of expectation. Their profession had not affected their hearts, and purified their lives. The passing of the time was well calculated to reveal such hearts. They were the first to turn and ridicule the sorrowful, disappointed ones, who really loved the appearing of their Saviour. I saw the wisdom of God in proving his people, and giving them a searching test to discover those who would shrink and turn back in the hour of trial.

Jesus and all the heavenly host looked with sympathy and love upon those who had with sweet expectation longed to see him whom their souls loved. Angels were hovering around them, to sustain them in the hour of their trial. Those who had neglected to receive the heavenly message were left in darkness, and God's anger was kindled against them, because they would not receive the light he had sent them from heaven. Those faithful, disappointed ones, who could not understand why their Lord did not come, were not left in darkness. Again they were led to their Bibles to search the prophetic periods. The hand of the Lord was removed from the figures, and the mistake was explained. They saw that the prophetic periods reached to 1844, and that the same evidence they had presented to show that the prophetic periods closed in 1843, proved that they would terminate in 1844. Light from the word of God shone upon their position, and they discovered a tarrying time. -- If the vision tarry, wait for it. -- In their love for Jesus' immediate coming, they had overlooked the tarrying of the vision, which was calculated to manifest the true waiting ones. Again they had a point of time. Yet I saw that many of them could not rise above their severe disappointment, to possess that degree of zeal and energy which had marked their faith in 1843.

Satan and his angels triumphed over them, and those who would not receive the message, congratulated themselves upon their far-seeing judgment and wisdom in not receiving the delusion, as they called it. They realized not that they were rejecting the counsel of God against themselves, and that they were working in union with Satan and his angels to perplex God's people, who were living out the heaven-born message.

The believers in this message were oppressed in the churches. Fear had held them for a time, so that they did not act out the sentiments of their heart, but the passing of the time revealed their true feelings. They wished to silence the testimony which the believers felt compelled to bear, that the prophetic periods extended to 1844. With clearness they explained their mistake, and gave their reasons why they expected their Lord in 1844. The opposers could not bring any arguments against the powerful reasons offered. The anger of the churches was kindled against them. They were determined not to listen to any evidence, and to shut their testimony out of the churches, so that others could not hear it. Those who dared not withhold from others the light God had given them, were shut out of the churches; but Jesus was with them, and they were joyful in the light of his countenance. They were prepared to receive the message of the second angel.

See Daniel 8:14; Habakkuk 2:1-4; Malachi chap. 3 & 4; Matthew 24:36; Revelation 14:6-7

CHAPTER 24

The Second Angel's Message

The churches would not receive the light of the first angel's message, and as they rejected the light from heaven they fell from the favor of God. They trusted in their own strength, and placed themselves by their opposition to the first message where they could not see the light of the second angel's message. But the beloved of God, who were oppressed, answered to the message, Babylon is fallen, and left the fallen churches.

Near the close of the second angel's message, I saw a great light from heaven shining upon the people of God. The rays of this light seemed bright as the sun. And I heard the voices of angels crying, Behold the Bridegroom cometh, go ye out to meet him!

The midnight cry was given to give power to the second angel's message. Angels were sent from heaven to wake up the discouraged saints, and prepare them for the great work before them. The most talented men were not the first to receive this message. Angels were sent to the humble, devoted ones, and constrained them to raise the cry, Behold the Bridegroom cometh, go ye out to meet him. Those entrusted with the cry made haste, and in the power of the Holy Spirit spread the cry, and aroused their discouraged brethren. This cry did not stand in the wisdom and learning of men, but in the power of God, and his saints who heard the cry could not resist it. The most spiritual received this message first, and those who had formerly led in the work were the last to receive and help swell the cry, Behold the Bridegroom cometh, go ye out to meet him.

In every part of the land, light was given upon the second angel's message, and the cry was melting down thousands. It went from city to city, and from village to village, until the waiting people of God were fully aroused. Many would not permit this message to enter the churches, and a large company who had the living testimony within them left the fallen churches. A mighty work was accomplished by the midnight cry. The message was heart-searching, and led the believers to seek a living experience for themselves. They knew that they could not lean upon one another.

The saints anxiously waited for their Lord with fasting, watching and almost constant prayer. Even some sinners looked forward to the time with terror, while the great mass seemed to be stirred against this message, and manifested the spirit of Satan. They mocked and scoffed, and everywhere was heard, No man knoweth the day and the hour. Evil angels exulted around them, urging them on to harden their hearts, and to reject every ray of light from heaven, that they might fasten them in the snare. Many professed to be looking for their Lord, who had neither part nor lot in the matter. The glory of God they had witnessed, the humility and deep devotion of the waiting ones, and the overwhelming weight of evidence, caused them to profess to receive the truth. But they were not converted. They were not ready. A spirit of solemn and earnest prayer was everywhere felt by the saints. A

65

holy solemnity was resting upon them. Angels with the deepest interest had watched the result, and were elevating those who received the heavenly message, and were drawing them from earthly things to obtain large supplies from salvation's fountain. God's people were then accepted with him. Jesus looked upon them with pleasure. His image was reflected in them. They had made a full sacrifice, an entire consecration, and expected to be changed to immortality. But they were destined to be again sadly disappointed. The time to which they looked, expecting deliverance, passed. They were still upon the earth, and the effects of the curse never seemed more visible. They had placed their affections on heaven, and in sweet anticipation, had tasted immortal deliverance; but their hopes were not realized.

The fear that had rested upon many of the people did not at once disappear. They did not immediately triumph over the disappointed ones. But as no visible wrath of God was felt by them, they recovered from the fear they had felt, and commenced their ridicule, their mocking, and scoffing. The people of God were again proved, and tested. The world laughed, and mocked, and reproached them; and those who had believed without a doubt that Jesus would then come and raise the dead, and change the living saints, and take the kingdom, and possess it forever, felt like the disciples of Christ. They have taken away my Lord, and I know not where they have laid him.

See Matthew 24:36, 25:6; John 20:13; Revelation 14:8

CHAPTER 25

Advent Movement Illustrated

I saw a number of companies who seemed to be bound together by cords. Many in these companies were in total darkness. Their eyes were directed downward to the earth, and there seemed to be no connection between them and Jesus. I saw individuals scattered through these different companies whose countenances looked light, and whose eyes were raised upward to heaven. Beams of light from Jesus, like rays of light from the sun, were imparted to them. An angel bid me look carefully, and I saw an angel watching over every one of those who had a ray of light, while evil angels surrounded those who were in darkness. I heard the voice of an angel cry, Fear God and give glory to him, for the hour of his judgment is come.

A glorious light rested down upon these companies, to enlighten all who would receive it. Some of those who were in darkness received the light and rejoiced; while others resisted the light from heaven, and said that it was deception to lead them astray. The light passed away from them, and they were left in darkness. Those who had received the light from Jesus, joyfully cherished the increase of precious light which was shed upon them. Their faces lighted up, and beamed with holy joy, while their gaze was directed upward to Jesus with intense interest, and their voices were heard in harmony with the voice of the angel, Fear God and give glory to him, for the hour of his judgment is come. As they raised this cry, I saw those who were in darkness thrusting them with side and with shoulder. Then many of those who cherished the sacred light, broke the cords which confined them, and stood out separate from those companies. And as many were breaking the cords which bound them, men belonging to these different companies, who were revered by them, passed through the companies, and some with pleasing words, and others with wrathful looks and threatening gestures, fastened the cords which were weakening, and were constantly saying, God is with us. We stand in the light. We have the truth. I inquired who these men were. I was told that they were ministers, and leading men, who had rejected the light themselves, and were unwilling that others should receive it. I saw those who cherished the light looking with interest and ardent desire upward, expecting Jesus to come and take them to himself. Soon a cloud passed over those who rejoiced in the light, and their faces looked sorrowful. I inquired the cause of this cloud. I was shown that it was their disappointment. The time when they expected their Saviour had passed, and Jesus had not come. Discouragement settled upon them, and those men I had before noticed, the ministers and leading men, rejoiced. Those who had rejected the light, triumphed greatly, while Satan and his evil angels also exulted around them.

Then I heard the voice of another angel, saying, Babylon is fallen! is fallen! A light shone upon those desponding ones, and with ardent desires for his appearing, they again fixed their eyes upon Jesus. Then I saw a number of angels conversing with the second angel, who had cried, Babylon is fallen, is fallen, and these angels raised their voices with the second angel, and cried, Behold the Bridegroom cometh! go ye out to meet him! The musical voices of these angels seemed to reach everywhere. An exceeding bright and glorious light shone around those who had cherished the light which had been imparted to them. Their faces shone with excellent glory, and they united with the angels in the cry, Behold, the Bridegroom cometh! And as they harmoniously raised the cry among these different companies, those who rejected the light, pushed them, and with angry looks, scorned and derided them. But the angels of God wafted their wings over the persecuted ones, while Satan and his angels were seeking to press their darkness around them, to lead them to reject the light from heaven.

Then I heard a voice saying to those who had been pushed and derided, come out from among them, and touch not the unclean. A large number broke the cords which bound them, and they obeyed the voice, and left those who were in darkness, and united with those who had previously broken the cords, and they joyfully united their voices with them. I heard the voice of earnest, agonizing prayer from a few who still remained with the companies who were in darkness. The ministers and leading men were passing around in these different companies, fastening the cords stronger; but still I heard this voice of earnest prayer. Then I saw those who had been praying reach out their hands for help towards that united company who were free, rejoicing in God. The answer from them, as they earnestly looked to heaven, and pointed upward, was, Come out from among them, and be separate. I saw individuals struggling for freedom, and at last they broke the cords that bound them. They resisted the efforts which were made to fasten the cords tighter, and would not heed the repeated assertions, God is with us, We have the truth with us. Individuals continued to leave the companies who were in darkness, and joined the free company, who appeared to be in an open field raised above the earth. Their gaze was upward, and the glory of God rested upon them, and they shouted the praises of God. They were united, and seemed to be wrapt in the light of heaven. Around this company were some who came under the influence of the light, but who were not particularly united to the company. All who cherished the light shed upon them were gazing upward with intense interest. Jesus looked upon them with sweet approbation. They expected Jesus to come. They longed for his appearing. They did not cast one lingering look to earth. Again I saw a cloud settle upon the waiting ones. I saw them turn their weary eyes downward. I inquired the cause of this change. Said my accompanying angel, They are again disappointed in their expectations. Jesus cannot yet come to earth. They must yet suffer for Jesus and endure greater trials. They must give up errors and traditions received from men, and turn wholly to God and his word. They must be purified, made white and tried. And those who endure that bitter trial will obtain an eternal victory.

Jesus did not come to earth as the waiting, joyful company expected, to cleanse the Sanctuary, by purifying the earth by fire. I saw that they were correct in their reckoning of the prophetic periods. Prophetic time closed in 1844. Their mistake consisted in not understanding what the Sanctuary was, and the nature of its cleansing. Jesus did enter the Most Holy place to cleanse the Sanctuary at the ending of the days. I looked again at the waiting, disappointed company. They looked sad. They carefully examined the evidences of their faith, and followed down through the reckoning of the prophetic periods, and could discover no mistake. Time was fulfilled, but where was their Saviour? They had lost him.

I was then shown the disappointment of the disciples as they came to the sepulchre and found not the body of Jesus. Said Mary, They have taken away my Lord, and I know not where they have laid him. Angels told the sorrowing disciples that their Lord had risen, and would go before them into Galilee.

I saw that as Jesus looked upon the disappointed ones with the deepest compassion, he sent his angels to direct their minds that they might find him, and follow him where he was; that they might understand that the earth is not the Sanctuary; that he must needs enter the Most Holy place of the heavenly Sanctuary to cleanse it; to make a special atonement for Israel, and to receive the kingdom of his Father, and then return to earth and take them to dwell with him forever. The disappointment of the disciples well represents the disappointment of those who expected their Lord in 1844. I was carried back to the time when Christ triumphantly rode into Jerusalem. The joyful disciples believed that he was then to take the kingdom, and reign a temporal prince. They followed their King with high hopes. They cut down the beautiful palm branches, and took off their outer garments, and with enthusiastic zeal spread them in the way; and some went before, and others followed crying, Hosanna to the Son of David! Blessed is he that cometh in the name of the Lord! Hosanna in the highest! The excitement disturbed the Pharisees, and they wished Jesus to rebuke his disciples. But he said unto them, If these should hold their peace, the stones would immediately cry out. The prophecy of Zechariah 9:9, must be fulfilled, yet, I saw, the disciples were doomed to a bitter disappointment. In a few days they followed Jesus to Calvary, and beheld him bleeding and mangled upon the cruel cross. They witnessed his agonizing death, and laid him in the tomb. Their hearts sunk with grief. Their expectations were not realized in a single particular. Their hopes died with Jesus. But as he arose from the dead, and appeared to his sorrowing disciples, their hopes revived. They had lost their Saviour; but again they had found him.

I saw that the disappointment of those who believed in the coming of the Lord in 1844, was not equal to the disappointment of the disciples. Prophecy was fulfilled in the first and second angels' messages. They were given at the right time, and accomplished the work God designed they should.

See Daniel 8:14; Matthew 21:4-16, 25:6; Mark 16:6-7; Luke 19:35-40; John 14:1-3, 20:13; 2 Corinthians 6:17; Revelation 10:8-11, 14:7-8

CHAPTER 26

Another Illustration

I was shown the interest which all heaven had taken in the work which had been going on upon the earth. Jesus commissioned a strong and mighty angel to descend and warn the inhabitants of earth to get ready for his second appearing. I saw the mighty angel leave the presence of Jesus in heaven. Before him went an exceedingly bright and glorious light. I was told that his mission was to lighten the earth with his glory, and warn man of the coming wrath of God. Multitudes received the light. Some seemed to be very solemn, while others were joyful and enraptured. The light was shed upon all, but some merely came under the influence of the light, and did not heartily receive it. But all who received it, turned their faces upward to heaven, and glorified God. Many were filled with great wrath. Ministers and people united with the vile, and stoutly resisted the light shed by the mighty angel. But all who received it withdrew from the world, and were closely united together.

Satan and his angels were busily engaged in seeking to attract the minds of all they could from the light. The company who rejected it were left in darkness. I saw the angel watching with the deepest interest the professed people of God, to record the character they developed, as the message of heavenly origin was introduced to them. And as very many who professed love for Jesus turned from the heavenly message with scorn, derision and hatred, an angel with a parchment in his hand, made the shameful record. All heaven was filled with indignation, because Jesus was slighted by his professed followers.

I saw the disappointment of the trusting ones. They did not see their Lord at the expected time. It was God's purpose to conceal the future, and bring his people to a point of decision. Without this point of time the work designed of God would not have been accomplished. Satan was leading the minds of very many far ahead in the future. A period of time proclaimed for Christ's appearing must bring the mind to earnestly seek for a present preparation. As the time passed, those who had not fully received the light of the angel, united with those who had despised the heavenly message, and they turned upon the disappointed ones in ridicule. I saw the angels in heaven consulting with Jesus. They had marked the situation of Christ's professed followers. The passing of the definite time had tested and proved them, and very many were weighed in the balance and found wanting. They all loudly professed to be Christians, yet failed in following Christ in almost every particular. Satan exulted at the state of the professed followers of Christ. He had them in his snare. He had led the majority to leave the straight path, and they were attempting to climb up to heaven some other way. Angels saw the pure, the clean, and holy, all mixed up with sinners in Zion, and the world-loving hypocrite. They had watched over the true lovers of Jesus; but the corrupt were affecting the holy.

Those whose hearts burned with a longing, intense desire to see Jesus, were forbidden by their professed brethren to speak of his coming. Angels viewed the whole scene, and sympathized with the remnant, who loved the appearing of Jesus. Another mighty angel was commissioned to descend to earth. Jesus placed in his hand a writing, and as he came to earth, he cried, Babylon is fallen! is fallen! Then I saw the disappointed ones again look cheerful, and raise their eyes to heaven, looking with faith and hope for their Lord's appearing. But many seemed to remain in a stupid state, as if asleep; yet I could see the trace of deep sorrow upon their countenances. The disappointed ones saw from the Bible that they were in the tarrying time, and that they must patiently wait the fulfillment of the vision. The same evidence which led them to look for their Lord in 1843, led them to expect him in 1844. I saw that the majority did not possess that energy which marked their faith in 1843. Their disappointment had dampened their faith. But as the disappointed ones united in the cry of the second angel, the heavenly host looked with the deepest interest, and marked the effect of the message. They saw those who bore the name of Christians turn with derision and scorn upon those who had been disappointed. As the words fell from the mocker's lips, You have not gone up yet! an angel wrote them. Said the angel, They mock God.

I was pointed back to the translation of Elijah. His mantle fell on Elisha, and wicked children (or young people) followed him, mocking, crying, Go up thou bald head! Go up thou bald head! They mocked God, and met their punishment there. They had learned it of their parents. And those who have scoffed and mocked at the idea of the saints' going up, will be visited with the plagues of God, and will realize that it is not a small thing to trifle with him.

Jesus commissioned other angels to fly quickly to revive and strengthen the drooping faith of his people, and prepare them to understand the message of the second angel, and of the important move which was soon to be made in heaven. I saw these angels receive great power and light from Jesus, and fly quickly to earth to fulfill their commission to aid the second angel in his work. A great light shone upon the people of God as the angels cried, Behold the Bridegroom cometh, go ye out to meet him. Then I saw those disappointed ones rise, and in harmony with the second angel, proclaim, Behold the Bridegroom cometh, go ye out to meet him. The light from the angels penetrated the darkness everywhere. Satan and his angels sought to hinder this light from spreading, and having its designed effect. They contended with the angels of God, and told them that God had deceived the people, and that with all their light and power, they could not make the people believe that Jesus was coming. The angels of God continued their work, although Satan strove to hedge up the way, and draw the minds of the people from the light. Those who received it looked very happy. They fixed their eyes up to heaven, and longed for the appearing of Jesus. Some were in great distress, weeping and praying. Their eyes seemed to be fixed upon themselves, and they dared not look upward.

A precious light from heaven parted the darkness from them, and their eyes, which had been fixed in despair upon themselves, were turned upward, while gratitude and holy joy were expressed upon every feature. Jesus and all the angelic host looked with approbation upon the faithful, waiting ones.

Those who rejected and opposed the light of the first angel's message, lost the light of the second, and could not be benefited by the power and glory which attended the message, Behold the Bridegroom cometh. Jesus turned from them with a frown. They had slighted and rejected him. Those who received the message were wrapt in a cloud of glory. They waited and watched and prayed to know the will of God. They greatly feared to offend him. I saw Satan and his angels seeking to shut this divine light from the people of God; but as long as the waiting ones cherished the light, and kept their eyes raised from earth to Jesus, Satan could have no power to deprive them of this precious light. The message given from heaven enraged Satan and his angels, and those who professed to love Jesus, but despised his coming, scorned and derided the faithful, trusting ones. But an angel marked every insult, every slight, every abuse they received from their professed brethren. Very many raised their voices to cry, Behold the Bridegroom cometh, and left their brethren who did not love the appearing of Jesus, and who would not suffer them to dwell upon his second coming. I saw Jesus turn his face from those who rejected and despised his coming, and then he bade angels lead his people out from among the unclean, lest they should be defiled. Those obedient to the messages stood out free and united. A holy and excellent light shone upon them. They renounced the world, tore their affections from it, and sacrificed their earthly interests. They gave up their earthly treasure and their anxious gaze was directed to heaven, expecting to see their loved Deliverer. A sacred, holy joy beamed upon their countenances, and told of the peace and joy which reigned within. Jesus bade his angels go and strengthen them, for the hour of their trial drew on. I saw that these waiting ones were not yet tried as they must be. They were not free from errors. And I saw the mercy and goodness of God in sending a warning to the people of earth, and repeated messages to bring them up to a point of time, to lead them to a diligent search of themselves, that they might divest themselves of errors which have been handed down from the heathen and papists. Through these messages God has been bringing out his people where he can work for them in greater power, and where they can keep all his commandments.

See 2Kings 2:11-25; Daniel 8:14; Habakkuk 2:1-4; Matthew 25:6; Revelation 14:8, 18:1-5

CHAPTER 27

The Sanctuary

I was then shown the grievous disappointment of the people of God. They did not see Jesus at the expected time. They knew not why their Saviour did not come. They could see no evidence why prophetic time had not ended. Said an angel, Has God's word failed? Has God failed to fulfill his promises? No: he has fulfilled all he promised. Jesus has risen up, and has shut the door of the Holy place of the heavenly Sanctuary, and has opened a door into the Most Holy place, and has entered in to cleanse the Sanctuary. Said the angel, All who wait patiently shall understand the mystery. Man has erred; but there has been no failure on the part of God. All was accomplished that God promised; but man erroneously looked to the earth, believing it to be the Sanctuary to be cleansed at the end of the prophetic periods. Man's expectations have failed; but God's promise not at all. Jesus sent his angels to direct the disappointed ones, to lead their minds into the Most Holy place where he had gone to cleanse the Sanctuary, and make a special atonement for Israel. Jesus told the angels that all who found him would understand the work which he was to perform. I saw that while Jesus was in the Most Holy place he would be married to the New Jerusalem, and after his work should be accomplished in the Holiest, he would descend to earth in kingly power and take the precious ones to himself who had patiently waited his return.

I was then shown what did take place in heaven as the prophetic periods ended in 1844. I saw that as the ministration of Jesus in the Holy place ended, and he closed the door of that apartment, a great darkness settled upon those who had heard, and had rejected the messages of Christ's coming, and they lost sight of him. Jesus then clothed himself with precious garments. Around the bottom of his robe was a bell and a pomegranate, a bell and a pomegranate. He had suspended from his shoulders a breastplate of curious work. And as he moved, it glittered like diamonds, magnifying letters which looked like names written, or engraven upon the breastplate. After he was fully attired, with something upon his head which looked like a crown, angels surrounded him, and in a flaming chariot he passed within the second vail. I was then bid to take notice of the two apartments of the heavenly Sanctuary. The curtain, or door, was opened, and I was permitted to enter. In the first apartment I saw the candlestick with seven lamps, which looked rich and glorious; also the table on which was the shew-bread, and the altar of incense, and the censer. All the furniture of this apartment looked like purest gold, and reflected the image of the one who entered that place. The curtain which separated these two apartments looked glorious. It was of different colors and material, with a beautiful border, with figures of gold wrought upon it, representing angels. The vail was lifted, and I looked into the second apartment. I saw there an ark which had the appearance of being of the finest gold. As a border around the top of the ark, was most beautiful work representing crowns. It was of fine gold. In the ark were the tables of stone containing the ten commandments. On each end of the ark was a lovely cherub with their wings spread out over it. Their wings were raised on high, and touched each other above the head of Jesus, as he stood by the ark. Their faces were turned towards each other, and they looked downwards to the ark, representing all the angelic host looking with interest at the law of God. Between the cherubim was a golden censer. And as the prayers of the saints in faith came up to Jesus, and he offered them to his Father, a sweet fragrance arose from the incense. It looked like smoke of most beautiful colors. Above the place where Jesus stood, before the ark, I saw an exceeding bright glory that I could not look upon. It appeared like a throne where God dwelt. As the incense ascended up to the Father, the excellent glory came from the Father's throne to Jesus, and from Jesus it was shed upon those whose prayers had come up like sweet incense. Light and glory poured upon Jesus in rich abundance, and overshadowed the mercy-seat, and the train of the glory filled the temple. I could not long look upon the glory. No language can describe it. I was overwhelmed, and turned from the majesty and glory of the scene.

I was shown a Sanctuary upon earth containing two apartments. It resembled the one in heaven. I was told that it was the earthly Sanctuary, a figure of the heavenly. The furniture of the first apartment of the earthly Sanctuary was like that in the first apartment of the heavenly. The vail was lifted, and I looked into the Holy of Holies, and saw that the furniture was the same as in the Most Holy place of the heavenly Sanctuary. The priests ministered in both apartments of the earthly. In the first apartment he ministered every day in the year, and entered the Most Holy but once in a year, to cleanse it from the sins which had been conveyed there. I saw that Jesus ministered in both apartments of the heavenly Sanctuary. He entered into the heavenly Sanctuary by the offering of his own blood. The earthly priests were removed by death, therefore they could not continue long; but Jesus, I saw, was a priest forever. Through the sacrifices and offerings brought to the earthly Sanctuary, the children of Israel were to lay hold of the merits of a Saviour to come. And in the wisdom of God the particulars of this work were given us that we might look back to them, and understand the work of Jesus in the heavenly Sanctuary.

At the crucifixion, as Jesus died on Calvary, he cried, It is finished, and the vail of the temple was rent in twain, from the top to the bottom. This was to show that the services of the earthly Sanctuary were forever finished, and that God would no more meet with them in their earthly temple, to accept their sacrifices. The blood of Jesus was then shed, which was to be ministered by himself in the heavenly Sanctuary. As the priests in the earthly Sanctuary entered the Most Holy once a year to cleanse the Sanctuary, Jesus entered the Most Holy of the heavenly, at the end of the 2300 days of Daniel 8, in 1844, to make a final atonement for all who could be benefited by his mediation, and to cleanse the Sanctuary.

 See Exodus chap.25-28; Leviticus chap.16; 2Kings 2:11; Daniel 8:14; Matthew 27:50-51; Hebrews chap.9; Revelation chap.21

CHAPTER 28

The Third Angel's Message

As the ministration of Jesus closed in the Holy place, and he passed into the Holiest, and stood before the ark containing the law of God, he sent another mighty angel to earth with the third message. He placed a parchment in the angel's hand, and as he descended to earth in majesty and power, he proclaimed a fearful warning, the most terrible threatening ever borne to man. This message was designed to put the children of God upon their guard, and show them the hour of temptation and anguish that was before them. Said the angel, They will be brought into close combat with the beast and his image. Their only hope of eternal life is to remain steadfast. Although their lives are at stake, yet they must hold fast the truth. The third angel closes his message with these words, Here is the patience of the saints; here are they that keep the commandments of God, and the faith of Jesus. As he repeated these words he pointed to the heavenly Sanctuary. The minds of all who embrace this message are directed to the Most Holy place where Jesus stands before the ark, making his final intercession for all those for whom mercy still lingers, and for those who have ignorantly broken the law of God. This atonement is made for the righteous dead as well as for the righteous living. Jesus makes an atonement for those who died, not receiving the light upon God's commandments, who sinned ignorantly.

After Jesus opened the door of the Most Holy the light of the Sabbath was seen, and the people of God were to be tested and proved, as God proved the children of Israel anciently, to see if they would keep his law. I saw the third angel pointing upward, showing the disappointed ones the way to the Holiest of the heavenly Sanctuary. They followed Jesus by faith into the Most Holy. Again they have found Jesus, and joy and hope spring up anew. I saw them looking back reviewing the past, from the proclamation of the second advent of Jesus, down through their travels to the passing of the time in 1844. They see their disappointment explained, and joy and certainty again animate them. The third angel has lighted up the past, present and future, and they know that God has indeed led them by his mysterious providence.

It was represented to me that the remnant followed Jesus into the Most Holy place, and beheld the ark, and the mercy-seat, and were captivated with their glory. Jesus raised the cover of the ark, and behold! the tables of stone, with the ten commandments written upon them. They trace down the lively oracles; but they start back with trembling when they see the fourth commandment living among the ten holy precepts, while a brighter light shines upon it than upon the other nine, and a halo of glory is all around it. They find nothing there informing them that the Sabbath has been abolished, or changed to the first day of the week. It reads as when spoken by the mouth of God in solemn and awful grandeur upon the mount, while the lightnings flashed and the thunders rolled, and when written with his own holy finger in the tables of stone. Six days shalt thou labor and do all thy work; but the seventh day is the Sabbath of the Lord thy God. They are amazed as they behold the care taken of the ten commandments. They see them placed close by Jehovah, overshadowed and protected by his holiness. They see that they have been trampling upon the fourth commandment of the decalogue, and have observed a day handed down by the heathen and papists, instead of the day sanctified by Jehovah. They humble themselves before God, and mourn over their past transgressions.

I saw the incense in the censer smoke as Jesus offered their confessions and prayers to his Father. And as it ascended, a bright light rested upon Jesus, and upon the mercy-seat; and the earnest, praying ones, who were troubled because they had discovered themselves to be transgressors of God's law, were blest, and their countenances lighted up with hope and joy. They joined in the work of the third angel, and raised their voices and proclaimed the solemn warning. But few at first received the message, yet they continued with energy to proclaim the warning. Then I saw many embrace the message of the third angel, and unite their voices with those who had first proclaimed the warning, and they exalted God and magnified him by observing his sanctified Rest-day.

Many who embraced the third message had not an experience in the two former messages. Satan understood this, and his evil eye was upon them to overthrow them; but the third angel was pointing them to the Most Holy place, and those who had an experience in the past messages were pointing them the way to the heavenly Sanctuary. Many saw the perfect chain of truth in the angels' messages, and gladly received it. They embraced them in their order, and followed Jesus by faith into the heavenly Sanctuary. These messages were represented to me as an anchor to hold the body. And as individuals receive and understand them, they are shielded against the many delusions of Satan.

After the great disappointment in 1844, Satan and his angels were busily engaged in laying snares to unsettle the faith of the body. He was affecting the minds of individuals who had a personal experience in these things. They had an appearance of humility. They changed the first and second messages, and pointed to the future for their fulfilment, while others pointed far back in the past, declaring that they had been there fulfilled. These individuals were drawing the minds of the inexperienced away, and unsettling their faith. Some were searching the Bible to try to build up a faith of their own, independent of the body. Satan exulted in all this; for he knew that those who broke loose from the anchor, he could affect by different errors and drive about with winds of doctrine. Many who had led in the first and second messages, denied them, and division and scattering was throughout the body. I then saw Wm. Miller. He looked perplexed, and was bowed with sorrow and distress for his people. He saw the company who were united and loving in 1844, losing their love for each other, and opposing one another. He saw them fall back into a cold, backslidden state. Grief wasted his strength. I saw leading men watching Wm. Miller, and fearing lest he should embrace the third angel's message and the commandments of God. And as he would lean towards the light from heaven, these men would lay some plan to draw his mind away. I saw a human influence exerted to keep his mind in darkness, and to retain his influence among them. At length Wm. Miller raised his voice against the light from heaven. He failed in not receiving the message which would have fully explained his disappointment, and cast a light and glory on the past, which would have revived his exhausted energies, brightened up his hope, and led him to glorify God. But he leaned to human wisdom instead of divine, and being broken with arduous labor in his Master's cause, and by age, he was not as accountable as those who kept him from the truth. They are responsible, and the sin rests upon them. If Wm. Miller could have seen the light of the third message, many things which looked dark and mysterious to him would have been explained. His brethren professed such deep love and interest for him, he thought he could not tear away from them. His heart would incline towards the truth; but then he looked at his brethren. They opposed it. Could he tear away from those who had stood side and shoulder with him in proclaiming Jesus' coming? He thought they surely would not lead him astray.

God suffered him to come under the power of Satan, and death to have dominion over him. He hid him in the grave, away from those who were constantly drawing him from God. Moses erred just as he was about to enter the promised land. So also, I saw that Wm. Miller erred as he was soon to enter the heavenly Canaan, in suffering his influence to go against the truth. Others led him to this. Others must account for it. But angels watch the precious dust of this servant of God, and he will come forth at the sound of the last trump.

See Exodus 20:1-17, 31:18; 1Thessalonians 4:16; Revelation 14:9-12

CHAPTER 29

A Firm Platform

I saw a company who stood well guarded and firm, and would give no countenance to those who would unsettle the established faith of the body. God looked upon them with approbation. I was shown three steps -- one, two and three -- the first, second and third angels' messages. Said the angel, Woe to him who shall move a block, or stir a pin in these messages. The true understanding of these messages is of vital importance. The destiny of souls hangs upon the manner in which they are received. I was again brought down through these messages, and saw how dearly the people of God had purchased their experience. It had been obtained through much suffering and severe conflict. Step by step had God brought them along, until he had placed them upon a solid, immovable platform. Then I saw individuals as they approached the platform, before stepping upon it examine the foundation. Some with rejoicing immediately stepped upon it. Others commenced to find fault with the laying of the foundation of the platform. They wished improvements made, and then the platform would be more perfect, and the people much happier. Some stepped off the platform and examined it, then found fault with it, declaring it to be laid wrong. I saw that nearly all stood firm upon the platform, and exhorted others who had stepped off to cease their complaints, for God was the master builder, and they were fighting against him. They recounted the wonderful work of God, which had led them to the firm platform, and in union nearly all raised their eyes to heaven, and with a loud voice glorified God. This affected some of those who had complained, and left the platform, and again they with humble look stepped upon it.

I was pointed back to the proclamation of the first advent of Christ. John was sent in the spirit and power of Elijah to prepare the way for Jesus' coming. Those who rejected the testimony of John were not benefited by the teachings of Jesus. Their opposition to the proclamation of his first advent placed them where they could not readily receive the strongest evidence of his being the Messiah. Satan led on those who rejected the message of John to go still further, to reject Jesus and crucify him. In doing this, they placed themselves where they could not receive the blessing on the day of Pentecost, which would have taught them the way into the heavenly Sanctuary. The rending of the vail of the temple showed that the Jewish sacrifices and ordinances would no longer be received. The great Sacrifice had been offered, and had been accepted, and the Holy Spirit which descended on the day of Pentecost carried the minds of the disciples from the earthly Sanctuary to the heavenly, where Jesus had entered by his own blood, and shed upon his disciples the benefits of his atonement. The Jews were left in complete deception and total darkness. They lost all the light they might have had upon the plan of salvation, and still trusted in their useless sacrifices and offerings. They could not be benefited by the mediation of Christ in the Holy place. The heavenly Sanctuary had taken the place of the earthly, yet they had no knowledge of the way to the heavenly.

Many look with horror at the course the Jews pursued toward Jesus in rejecting and crucifying him. And as they read the history of his shameful abuse, they think they love Christ, and would not have denied him like Peter, or crucified him like the Jews. But God who has witnessed their professed sympathy for his Son, has proved them, and has brought to the test that love which they professed for Jesus.

All heaven watched with the deepest interest the reception of the message. But many who profess to love Jesus, and who shed tears as they read the story of the cross, instead of receiving the message with gladness, are stirred with anger, and deride the good news of Jesus' coming, and declare it to be delusion. They would not fellowship those who loved his appearing, but hated them, and shut them out of the churches. Those who rejected the first message could not be benefited by the second, and were not benefited by the midnight cry, which was to prepare them to enter with Jesus by faith into the Most Holy place of the heavenly Sanctuary. And by rejecting the two former messages, they can see no light in the third angel's message, which shows the way into the Most Holy place. I saw that the nominal churches, as the Jews crucified Jesus, had crucified these messages, and therefore they have no knowledge of the move made in heaven, or of the way into the Most Holy, and they cannot be benefited by the intercession of Jesus there. Like the Jews, who offered their useless sacrifices, they offer up their useless prayers to the apartment which Jesus has left, and Satan, pleased with the deception of the professed followers of Christ, fastens them in his snare, and assumes a religious character, and leads the minds of these professed Christians to himself, and works with his power, his signs and lying wonders. Some he deceives in one way and some in another. He has different delusions prepared to affect different minds. Some look with horror upon one deception, while they readily receive another. Satan deceives some with Spiritualism. He also comes as an angel of light, and spreads his influence over the land. I saw false reformations everywhere. The churches were elated, and considered that God was marvelously working for them, when it was another spirit. It will die away and leave the world and the church in a worse condition than before.

I saw that God had honest children among the nominal Adventists, and the fallen churches, and ministers and people will yet be called out from these churches, before the plagues shall be poured out, and they will gladly embrace the truth. Satan knows this, and before the loud cry of the third angel, raises an excitement in these religious bodies, that those who have rejected the truth may think God is with them. He hopes to deceive the honest, and lead them to think that God is still working for the churches. But the light will shine, and every one of the honest ones will leave the fallen churches, and take their stand with the remnant.

See Matthew chap. 3; Acts chap. 2; 2 Corinthians 11:14; 2 Thessalonians 2:9-12; Revelation 14:6-12

CHAPTER 30

Spiritualism

I saw the rapping delusion. Satan has power to bring the appearance of forms before us purporting to be our relatives and friends that now sleep in Jesus. It will be made to appear as if they were present, the words they uttered while here, which we were familiar with, will be spoken, and the same tone of voice which they had while living will fall upon the ear. All this is to deceive the world, and ensnare them into the belief of this delusion.

I saw that the saints must have a thorough understanding of the present truth, which they will have to maintain from the Scriptures. They must understand the state of the dead; for the spirits of devils will yet appear to them, professing to be beloved friends and relatives, who will declare to them unscriptural doctrines. They will do all in their power to excite sympathy, and work miracles before them, to confirm what they declare. The people of God must be prepared to withstand these spirits with the Bible truth that the dead know not anything, and that they are the spirits of devils.

I saw that we must examine well the foundation of our hope, for we shall have to give a reason for it from the Scriptures; for we shall see this delusion spreading, and we shall have to contend with it face to face. And unless we are prepared for it, we shall be ensnared and overcome. But if we do what we can on our part to be ready for the conflict that is just before us, God will do his part, and his all-powerful arm will protect us. He would sooner send every angel out of glory to make a hedge about faithful souls, than that they should be deceived and led away by the lying wonders of Satan.

I saw the rapidity with which this delusion was spreading. A train of cars was shown me, going with the speed of lightning. The angel bade me look carefully. I fixed my eyes upon the train. It seemed that the whole world was on board. Then he showed me the conductor, who looked like a stately fair person, whom all the passengers looked up to and reverenced. I was perplexed, and asked my attending angel who it was. Said he, It is Satan. He is the conductor in the form of an angel of light. He has taken the world captive. They are given over to strong delusions, to believe a lie that they may be damned. His agent, the next highest in order to him, is the engineer, and others of his agents are employed in different offices as he may need them, and they are all going with lightning speed to perdition. I asked the angel if there were none left. He bade me look in an opposite direction, and I saw a little company traveling a narrow pathway. All seemed to be firmly united, and bound together by the truth.

This little company looked care-worn, as though they had passed through severe trials and conflicts. And it seemed as if the sun had just appeared from behind the cloud, and shone upon their countenances, and caused them to look triumphant, as though their victories were nearly won.

I saw that the Lord had given the world opportunity to discover the snare. This one thing was evidence enough for the Christian if there were no other. There is no difference made between the precious and the vile.

Thomas Paine, whose body has mouldered to dust, and who is to be called forth at the end of the 1000 years, at the second resurrection, to receive his reward, and suffer the second death, is purported by Satan to be in heaven, and highly exalted there. Satan used him on earth as long as he could, and now he is carrying on the same work through pretensions of having Thomas Paine so much exalted and honored; and as he taught on earth, Satan is making it appear that he is teaching in heaven. And some on earth who have looked with horror at his life and death, and his corrupt teachings while living, now submit to be taught by him who was one of the vilest and most corrupt of men; one who despised God and his law.

He who is the father of lies, blinds and deceives the world by sending his angels forth to speak for apostles, and make it appear that they contradict what they wrote when on earth, which was dictated by the Holy Ghost. These lying angels make the apostles to corrupt their own teachings and declare them to be adulterated. By so doing he can throw professed Christians, who have a name to live and are dead, and all the world, into uncertainty about the word of God; for that cuts directly across his track, and is likely to thwart his plans. Therefore he gets them to doubt the divine origin of the Bible, and then sets up the infidel Thomas Paine, as though he was ushered into heaven when he died, and with the holy apostles whom he hated on earth, is united, and appears to be teaching the world.

Satan assigns each one of his angels their part to act. He enjoins upon them to be cunning, artful and sly. He instructs some of them to act the part of the apostles, and speak for them, while others are to act out infidels and wicked men who died cursing God, but now appear to be very religious. There is no difference made between the most holy apostles and the vilest infidel. They are both made to teach the same thing. It matters not who Satan makes to speak, if his object is only accomplished. He was so intimately connected with Paine upon earth, and so aided him, that it is an easy thing for him to know the very words he used, and the very hand-writing of one of his devoted children who served him so faithfully, and accomplished his purposes so well. Satan dictated much of his writings, and it is an easy thing for him to dictate sentiments through his angels now, and make it appear that it comes through Thomas Paine, who was his devoted servant while he lived. But this is the masterpiece of Satan. All this teaching purporting to be from apostles, and saints, and wicked men who have died, comes directly from his Satanic majesty.

This should be enough to remove the vail from every mind and discover unto all the dark, mysterious works of Satan; -- that he has got one whom he loved so well, and who hated God so perfectly, with the holy apostles and angels in glory: virtually saying to the world and infidels, No matter how wicked you are; no matter whether you believe in God or the Bible, or disbelieve; live as you please, heaven is your home; -- for everyone knows that if Thomas Paine is in heaven, and so exalted, they will surely get there. This is so glaring that all may see if they will. Satan is doing now what he has been trying to do since his fall, through individuals like Thomas Paine. He is, through his power and lying wonders, tearing away the foundation of the Christians' hope, and putting out their sun that is to lighten them in the narrow way to heaven. He is making the world believe that the Bible is no better than a story-book, uninspired, while he holds out something to take its place; namely, *Spiritual Manifestations*!

Here is a channel wholly devoted to himself, under his control, and he can make the world believe what he will. The Book that is to judge him and his followers, he puts back into the shade, just where he wants it. The Saviour of the world he makes to be no more than a common man; and as the Roman guard that watched the tomb of Jesus, spread the false and lying report that the chief priests and elders put in their mouth, so will the poor, deluded followers of these pretended spiritual manifestations, repeat, and try to make it appear, that there is nothing miraculous about our Saviour's birth, death and resurrection; and they put Jesus with the Bible, back into the shade, where they want him, and then get the world to look to them and their lying wonders and miracles, which they declare far exceed the works of Christ. Thus the world is taken in the snare, and lulled to security; not to find out their awful deception, until the seven last plagues are poured out. Satan laughs as he sees his plan succeed so well, and the whole world in the snare.

See Ecclesiastes 9:5; John 11:1-45; 2 Thessalonians 2:9-12; Revelation 13:3-14

CHAPTER 31

Covetousness

I saw Satan and his angels consulting together. He bade his angels go and lay their snares especially for those who were looking for Christ's second appearing, and who were keeping all God's commandments. Satan told his angels that the churches were all asleep. He would increase his power and lying wonders, and he could hold them. But the sect of Sabbath-keepers we hate. They are continually working against us, and taking from us our subjects, to keep that hated law of God.

Go, make the possessors of lands and money drunk with cares. If you can make them place their affections upon these things, we have them yet. They may profess what they please, only make them care more for money than the success of Christ's kingdom, or the spread of the truths we hate. Present the world before them in the most attractive light, that they may love and idolize it. We must keep all the means in our ranks we can. The more means they have, the more will they injure our kingdom by getting our subjects. And as they appoint meetings in different places, then we are in danger. Be very vigilant then. Cause all the distraction you can. Destroy love for each other. Discourage and dishearten their ministers; for we hate them. Hold up every plausible excuse to those that have means, lest they hand it out. Control the money matters if you can, and drive their ministers to want, and distress. This will weaken their courage and zeal. Battle every inch of ground. Make covetousness and love of earthly treasures the ruling traits of their character. As long as these traits rule, salvation and grace stand back. Crowd all you can around them to attract them, and they will be surely ours. Not only are we sure of them, but their hateful influence will not be exercised toward others to lead them to heaven. And those who shall attempt to give, put within them a grudging disposition, that it may be sparingly.

I saw that Satan carried out his plans well. And as the servants of God appointed meetings, Satan and his angels understood their business, and were on the ground to hinder the work of God, and he was constantly putting suggestions into the minds of God's people. Some he leads in one way, and some in another, always taking advantage of evil traits in the brethren and sisters, exciting and stirring up their natural besetments. If they are disposed to be selfish and covetous, Satan is well pleased to take his stand by their side, and then with all his power he seeks to lead them to manifest their besetting sins. If the grace of God and the light of truth melt away these covetous, selfish feelings for a little, and they do not obtain entire victory over them, when they are not under a saving influence, Satan comes in and withers up every noble, generous principle, and they think that they have to do too much. They become weary of well-doing and forget all about the great sacrifice Jesus made for them, to redeem them from the power of Satan, and hopeless misery.

Satan took advantage of Judas' covetous, selfish disposition, and led him to murmur against the ointment Mary dedicated to Jesus. Judas looked upon it as a great waste; it might have been sold and given to the poor. He cared not for the poor, but considered the liberal offering to Jesus extravagant. Judas prized his Lord just enough to sell him for a few pieces of silver. And I saw that there were some like Judas among those who profess to be waiting for their Lord. Satan has the control over them, but they know it not. Not a particle of covetousness or selfishness can God approbate. He hates it, and he despises the prayers and exhortations of those who possess it. As Satan sees his time is short, he leads them on to be more and more selfish, more and more covetous, and then exults as he sees them wrapt up in themselves, close, penurious and selfish. If the eyes of such could be opened, they would see Satan in hellish triumph, exulting over them, and laughing at the folly of those who accept his suggestions, and enter his snares. Then he and his angels take the mean and covetous acts of these individuals, and present them to Jesus and the holy angels, and reproachfully say, These are Christ's followers! They are getting ready to be translated! Satan marks their deviating course, and then compares it with the Bible, with passages which plainly rebuke such things, and then presents it to annoy the heavenly angels, saying, These are following Christ and his word! These are the fruits of Christ's sacrifice and redemption! Angels turn in disgust from the scene. God requires a constant doing on the part of his people, and when they become weary of well and generous doing, he becomes weary of them. I saw that God was greatly displeased with the least manifestation of selfishness on the part of his professed people, for whom Jesus has not spared his own precious life. Every selfish, covetous individual will fall out by the way. Like Judas, who sold his Lord, they will sell good principles, and a noble, generous disposition for a little of earth's gain. All such will be sifted out from God's people. Those who want heaven, must, with every energy they possess, be encouraging the principles of heaven. And instead of their souls withering up with selfishness, they should be expanding with benevolence, and every opportunity should be improved in doing good to one another, and increasing and growing more and more into the principles of heaven. Jesus was held up to me as the perfect pattern. His life was without selfish interest, and was marked with disinterested benevolence.

See Mark 14:3-11; Luke 12:15-40; Colossians 3:5-16; 1 John 2:15-17

CHAPTER 32

The Shaking

I saw some with strong faith and agonizing cries, pleading with God. Their countenances were pale, and marked with deep anxiety, which expressed their internal struggle. There were firmness and great earnestness expressed in their countenances, while large drops of perspiration rose upon their foreheads, and fell. Now and then their faces would light up with the marks of God's approbation, and again the same solemn, earnest, anxious look settled upon them.

Evil angels crowded around them, pressing their darkness upon them, to shut out Jesus from their view, that their eyes might be drawn to the darkness that surrounded them, and they distrust God, and next murmur against him. Their only safety was in keeping their eyes directed upward. Angels were having the charge over the people of God, and as the poisonous atmosphere from these evil angels was pressed around these anxious ones, the angels, which had the charge over them, were continually wafting their wings over them to scatter the thick darkness that surrounded them.

Some, I saw, did not participate in this work of agonizing and pleading. They seemed indifferent and careless. They were not resisting the darkness around them, and it shut them in like a thick cloud. The angels of God left them, and went to the aid of those earnest, praying ones. I saw the angels of God hasten to the assistance of all those who were struggling with all their energies to resist those evil angels, and trying to help themselves by calling upon God with perseverance. But the angels left those who made no effort to help themselves, and I lost sight of them.

As these praying ones continued their earnest cries, at times a ray of light from Jesus came to them, and encouraged their hearts, and lighted up their countenances.

I asked the meaning of the shaking I had seen. I was shown that it would be caused by the straight testimony called forth by the counsel of the true Witness to the Laodiceans. It will have its effect upon the heart of the receiver of the testimony, and it will lead him to exalt the standard and pour forth the straight truth. This straight testimony some will not bear. They will rise up against it, and this will cause a shaking among God's people.

I saw that the testimony of the true Witness has not been half heeded. The solemn testimony upon which the destiny of the church hangs, has been lightly esteemed, if not entirely disregarded. This testimony must work deep repentance, and all that truly receive it, will obey it, and be purified.

Said the angel, List ye! Soon I heard a voice that sounded like many musical instruments, all sounding in perfect strains, sweet and harmonious. It surpassed any music I had ever heard. It seemed to be so full of mercy, compassion, and elevating, holy joy. It thrilled through my whole being. Said the angel, Look ye! My attention was then turned to the company I had seen before, who were mightily shaken. I was shown those whom I had before seen weeping, and praying with agony of spirit. I saw that the company of guardian angels around them had doubled, and they were clothed with an armor from their head to their feet. They moved in exact order, firm like a company of soldiers. Their countenances expressed the severe conflict which they had endured, the agonizing struggle they had passed through. Yet their features, marked with severe internal anguish, shone now with the light and glory of heaven. They had obtained the victory, and it called forth from them the deepest gratitude, and holy, sacred joy.

The numbers of this company had lessened. Some had been shaken out, and left by the way. The careless and indifferent who did not join with those who prized victory and salvation enough to agonize, persevere, and plead for it, did not obtain it, and they were left behind in darkness, and their numbers were immediately made up by others taking hold of the truth, and coming into the ranks. Still the evil angels pressed around them, but they could have no power over them.

I heard those clothed with the armor speak forth the truth in great power. It had effect. I saw those who had been bound; some wives had been bound by their husbands, and some children had been bound by their parents. The honest who had been held or prevented from hearing the truth, now eagerly laid hold of the truth spoken. All fear of their relatives was gone. The truth alone was exalted to them. It was dearer and more precious than life. They had been hungering and thirsting for truth. I asked what had made this great change. An angel answered, It is the latter rain; the refreshing from the presence of the Lord; the loud cry of the third angel.

Great power was with these chosen ones. Said the angel, Look ye! My attention was turned to the wicked, or unbelievers. They were all astir. The zeal and power with the people of God had aroused and enraged them. Confusion, confusion, was on every side. I saw measures taken against this company, who were having the power and light of God. Darkness thickened around them, yet there they stood, approved of God, and trusting in him. I saw them perplexed. Next I heard them crying unto God earnestly. Through the day and night their cry ceased not. I heard these words, Thy will, O God, be done! If it can glorify thy name, make a way of escape for thy people! Deliver us from the heathen round about us! They have appointed us unto death; but thine arm can bring salvation. These are all the words I can bring to mind. They seemed to have a deep sense of their unworthiness, and manifested entire submission to the will of God. Yet everyone, without an exception, was earnestly pleading, and wrestling like Jacob for deliverance.

Soon after they had commenced their earnest cry, the angels, in sympathy would have gone to their deliverance. But a tall, commanding angel suffered them not. Said he, The will of God is not yet fulfilled. They must drink of the cup. They must be baptized with the baptism.

Soon I heard the voice of God, which shook the heavens and the earth. There was a mighty earthquake. Buildings were shaken down, and fell on every side. I then heard a triumphant shout of victory, loud, musical and clear. I looked upon this company who, a short time before were in such distress and bondage. Their captivity was turned. A glorious light shone upon them. How beautiful they then looked. All weariness and marks of care were gone. Health and beauty were seen in every countenance. Their enemies, the heathen around them, fell like dead men. They could not endure the light that shone upon the delivered, holy ones. This light and glory remained upon them, until Jesus was seen in the clouds of heaven, and the faithful, tried company was changed in a moment, in the twinkling of an eye, from glory to glory. And the graves were opened and the saints came forth, clothed with immortality, crying victory over death and the grave, and together with the living saints, were caught up to meet their Lord in the air; while the rich, musical shouts of glory and victory were upon every immortal tongue, and proceeding from every sanctified, holy lip.

See Psalms chap.86; Hosea 6:3; Haggai 2:21-23; Matthew 10:35-39, 20:23; Ephesians 6:10-18; 1Thessalonians 4:14-18; Revelation 3:14-22

CHAPTER 33

The Sins of Babylon

I saw the state of the different churches since the second angel proclaimed their fall. They have been growing more and more corrupt; yet they bear the name of being Christ's followers. It is impossible to distinguish them from the world. Their ministers take their text from the Word, but preach smooth things. The natural heart feels no objection to this. It is only the spirit and power of the truth, and the salvation of Christ, that is hateful to the carnal heart. There is nothing in the popular ministry that stirs the wrath of Satan, makes the sinner tremble, or applies to the heart and conscience the fearful realities of a judgment soon to come. Wicked men are generally pleased with a form without true godliness, and they will aid and support such a religion. Said the angel, Nothing less than the whole armor of righteousness can overcome, and retain the victory over the powers of darkness. Satan has taken full possession of the churches as a body. The sayings and doings of men are dwelt upon instead of the plain cutting truths of the word of God. Said the angel, The friendship and spirit of the world are at enmity with God. When truth in its simplicity and strength, as it is in Jesus, is brought to bear against the spirit of the world, it awakens the spirit of persecution at once. Many, very many, who profess to be Christians, have not known God. The character of the natural heart has not been changed, and the carnal mind remains at enmity with God. They are Satan's own faithful servants, notwithstanding they have assumed another name.

I saw that since Jesus had left the Holy place of the heavenly Sanctuary, and had entered within the second vail, the churches were left as were the Jews; and they have been filling up with every unclean and hateful bird. I saw great iniquity and vileness in the churches; yet they profess to be Christians. Their profession, their prayers and their exhortations, are an abomination in the sight of God. Said the angel, God will not smell in their assemblies. Selfishness, fraud and deceit are practiced by them without the reprovings of conscience. And over all these evil traits they throw the cloak of religion. I was shown the pride of the nominal churches. God was not in their thoughts; but their carnal minds dwell upon themselves. They decorate their poor mortal bodies, and then look upon themselves with satisfaction and pleasure. Jesus and the angels looked upon them in anger. Said the angel, Their sins and pride have reached unto heaven. Their portion is prepared. Justice and judgment have slumbered long, but will soon awake. Vengeance is mine, and I will repay, saith the Lord. The fearful threatenings of the third angel are to be realized, and they will drink the wrath of God. An innumerable host of evil angels are spreading themselves over the whole land. The churches and religious bodies are crowded with them. And they look upon the religious bodies with exultation; for the cloak of religion covers the greatest crimes and iniquity.

All heaven beholds with indignation, human beings, the workmanship of God, reduced to the lowest depths of degradation, and placed on a level with the brute creation by their fellow men. And professed followers of that dear Saviour whose compassion was ever moved as he witnessed human woe, heartily engage in this enormous and grievous sin, and deal in slaves and souls of men. Angels have recorded it all. It is written in the book. The tears of the pious bond-men and bond-women, of fathers, mothers and children, brothers and sisters, are all bottled up in heaven. Agony, human agony, is carried from place to place, and bought and sold. God will restrain his anger but a little longer. His anger burns against this nation, and especially against the religious bodies who have sanctioned, and have themselves engaged in this terrible merchandise. Such injustice, such oppression, such sufferings, many professed followers of the meek and lowly Jesus can witness with heartless indifference. And many of them can inflict with hateful satisfaction, all this indescribable agony themselves, and yet dare to worship God. It is solemn mockery, and Satan exults over it, and reproaches Jesus and his angels with such inconsistency, saying, with hellish triumph, *Such are Christ's followers*!

These professed Christians read of the sufferings of the martyrs, and tears course down their cheeks. They wonder that men could ever possess hearts so hardened as to practice such inhuman cruelties towards their fellow-men, while at the same time they hold their fellow-men in slavery. And this is not all. They sever the ties of nature, and cruelly oppress from day to day their fellow-men. They can inflict most inhuman tortures with relentless cruelty, which would well compare with the cruelty papists and heathens exercised towards Christ's followers. Said the angel, It will be more tolerable for the heathen and for papists in the day of the execution of God's judgment than for such men. The cries and sufferings of the oppressed have reached unto heaven, and angels stand amazed at the hard-hearted, untold, agonizing suffering, man in the image of his Maker, causes his fellow-man. Said the angel, The names of such are written in blood, crossed with stripes, and flooded with agonizing, burning tears of suffering. God's anger will not cease until he has caused the land of light to drink the dregs of the cup of his fury, and until he has rewarded unto Babylon double. Reward her even as she rewarded you, double unto her double according to her works: in the cup which she hath filled, fill to her double.

I saw that the slave-master would have to answer for the soul of his slave whom he has kept in ignorance; and all the sins of the slave will be visited upon the master. God cannot take the slave to heaven, who has been kept in ignorance and degradation, knowing nothing of God, or the Bible, fearing nothing but his master's lash, and not holding so elevated a position as his master's brute beasts. But he does the best thing for him that a compassionate God can do. He lets him be as though he had not been; while the master has to suffer the seven last plagues, and then come up in the second resurrection, and suffer the second, most awful death. Then the wrath of God will be appeased.

See Amos 5:21; Romans 12:19; Revelation 14:9-10, 18:6

CHAPTER 34

The Loud Cry

I saw angels hurrying to and fro in heaven. They were descending to earth, and again ascending to heaven, preparing for the fulfilment of some important event. Then I saw another mighty angel commissioned to descend to earth, and unite his voice with the third angel, and give power and force to his message. Great power and glory were imparted to the angel, and as he descended, the earth was lightened with his glory. The light which went before and followed after this angel, penetrated everywhere, as he cried mightily, with a strong voice, saying, Babylon the great is fallen, is fallen, and is become the habitation of devils, and the hold of every foul spirit, and a cage of every unclean and hateful bird. The message of the fall of Babylon, as given by the second angel, is again given, with the addition of the corruptions which have been entering the churches since 1844. The work of this angel comes in at the right time, and joins in the last great work of the third angel's message, as it swells into a loud cry. And the people of God are fitted up everywhere to stand in the hour of temptation which they are soon to meet. I saw a great light resting upon them, and they united in the message, and fearlessly proclaimed with great power the third angel's message.

Angels were sent to aid the mighty angel from heaven, and I heard voices which seemed to sound everywhere, Come out of her, my people, that ye be not partakers of her sins, and that ye receive not of her plagues; for her sins have reached unto heaven, and God hath remembered her iniquities. This message seemed to be an addition to the third message, and joined it, as the midnight cry joined the second angel's message in 1844. The glory of God rested upon the patient, waiting saints, and they fearlessly gave the last solemn warning, proclaiming the fall of Babylon, and calling upon God's people to come out of her; that they might escape her fearful doom.

The light that was shed upon the waiting ones penetrated everywhere, and those who had any light in the churches, who had not heard and rejected the three messages, answered to the call, and left the fallen churches. Many had come to years of accountability since these messages had been given, and the light shone upon them, and they were privileged to choose life or death. Some chose life, and took their stand with those looking for their Lord, and keeping all his commandments. The third message was to do its work; all were to be tested upon it, and the precious ones were to be called out from the religious bodies. A compelling power moves the honest, while the manifestation of the power of God holds in fear and restraint relatives and friends, and they dare not, neither have they power to, hinder those who feel the work of the Spirit of God upon them. The last call is carried even to the poor slaves, and the pious among them, with humble expressions, pour forth their songs of extravagant joy at the prospect of their happy deliverance, and their masters cannot check them; for a fear and astonishment keep them silent. Mighty miracles are wrought, the sick are healed, and signs and wonders follow the believers. God is in the work, and every saint, fearless of consequences, follows the convictions of his own conscience, and unites with those who are keeping all the commandments of God; and they sound abroad the third message with power. I saw that the third message would close with power and strength far exceeding the midnight cry.

Servants of God, endowed with power from on high, with their faces lighted up, and shining with holy consecration, went forth fulfilling their work, and proclaiming the message from heaven. Souls that were scattered all through the religious bodies answered to the call, and the precious were hurried out of the doomed churches, as Lot was hurried out of Sodom before her destruction. God's people were fitted up and strengthened by the excellent glory which fell upon them in rich abundance, preparing them to endure the hour of temptation. A multitude of voices I heard everywhere, saying, Here is the patience of the saints; here are they that keep the commandments of God, and the faith of Jesus.

See Genesis chap.19; Revelation 14:12, 18:2-5

CHAPTER 35

The Third Message Closed

I was pointed down to the time when the third angel's message was closing. The power of God had rested upon his people. They had accomplished their work, and were prepared for the trying hour before them. They had received the latter rain, or refreshing from the presence of the Lord, and the living testimony had been revived. The last great warning had sounded everywhere, and it had stirred up and enraged the inhabitants of earth, who would not receive the message.

I saw angels hurrying to and fro in heaven. An angel returned from the earth with a writer's ink-horn by his side, and reported to Jesus that his work was done, that the saints were numbered and sealed. Then I saw Jesus, who had been ministering before the ark containing the ten commandments, throw down the censer. He raised his hands upward, and with a loud voice said, *It is done.* And all the angelic host laid off their crowns as Jesus made the solemn declaration, He that is unjust, let him be unjust still; and he which is filthy, let him be filthy still; and he that is righteous, let him be righteous still; and he that is holy, let him be holy still.

I saw that every case was then decided for life or death. Jesus had blotted out the sins of his people. He had received his kingdom, and the atonement had been made for the subjects of his kingdom. While Jesus had been ministering in the Sanctuary, the judgment had been going on for the righteous dead, and then for the righteous living. The subjects of the kingdom were made up. The marriage of the Lamb was finished. And the kingdom, and the greatness of the kingdom under the whole heaven, was given to Jesus, and the heirs of salvation, and Jesus was to reign as King of kings, and Lord of lords.

As Jesus moved out of the Most Holy place, I heard the tinkling of the bells upon his garment, and as he left, a cloud of darkness covered the inhabitants of the earth. There was then no mediator between guilty man, and an offended God. While Jesus had been standing between God and guilty man, a restraint was upon the people; but when Jesus stepped out from between man and the Father, the restraint was removed, and Satan had the control of man. It was impossible for the plagues to be poured out while Jesus officiated in the Sanctuary; but as his work there is finished, as his intercession closes, there is nothing to stay the wrath of God, and it breaks with fury upon the shelterless head of the guilty sinner, who has slighted salvation, and hated reproof. The saints in that fearful time, after the close of Jesus' mediation, were living in the sight of a holy God, without an intercessor. Every case was decided, every jewel numbered. Jesus tarried a moment in the outer apartment of the heavenly Sanctuary, and the sins which had been confessed while he was in the Most Holy place, he placed back upon the originator of sin, the Devil. He must suffer the punishment of these sins.

Then I saw Jesus lay off his priestly attire, and clothe himself with his most kingly robes -- upon his head were many crowns, a crown within a crown -- and surrounded by the angelic host, he left heaven. The plagues were falling upon the inhabitants of the earth. Some were denouncing God, and cursing him. Others rushed to the people of God, and begged to be taught how they should escape the judgments of God. But the saints had nothing for them. The last tear for sinners had been shed, the last agonizing prayer offered, the last burden had been borne. The sweet voice of mercy was no more to invite them. The last note of warning had been given. When the saints, and all heaven were interested for their salvation, they had no interest for themselves. Life and death had been set before them. Many desired life; but did not make any effort to obtain it. They did not choose life, and now there was no atoning blood to cleanse the sinner. No compassionate Saviour to plead for them, and cry, Spare, spare the sinner a little longer. All heaven had united with Jesus, as they heard the fearful words, It is done, It is finished. The plan of salvation had been accomplished. But few had chosen to accept the plan. And as mercy's sweet voice died away, a fearfulness and horror seized them. With terrible distinctness they hear, Too late! too late!

Those who had not prized God's word were hurrying to and fro. They wandered from sea to sea, and from the north to the east, to seek the word of the Lord. Said the angel, They shall not find it. There is a famine in the land; not a famine of bread, nor a thirst for water, but of hearing the words of the Lord. What would they not give for one word of approval from God? but no, they must hunger and thirst on. Day after day have they slighted salvation, and prized earthly pleasure, and earthly riches, higher than any heavenly inducement and treasure. They have rejected Jesus, and despised his saints. The filthy must remain filthy forever.

A great portion of the wicked were greatly enraged, as they suffered the effects of the plagues. It was a scene of fearful agony. Parents were bitterly reproaching their children, and children reproaching their parents, brothers their sisters, and sisters their brothers. Loud wailing cries were heard in every direction, It was you who kept me from receiving the truth, which would have saved me from this awful hour. The people turned upon the ministers with bitter hate, and reproached them, telling them, You have not warned us. You told us all the world was to be converted, and cried, Peace, peace, to quiet every fear that was aroused. You have not told us of this hour, and those who warned us of it you said were fanatics, and evil men, who would ruin us. But the ministers, I saw, did not escape the wrath of God. Their sufferings were ten-fold greater than their people's.

See Ezekiel 9:2-11; Daniel 7:27; Hosea 6:3; Amos 8:11-13; Revelation chap. 16, 17:14

CHAPTER 36

The Time of Jacob's Trouble

I saw the saints leaving the cities and villages, and associating in companies together, and living in the most solitary places. Angels provided them food and water; but the wicked were suffering with hunger and thirst. Then I saw the leading men of earth consulting together, and Satan and his angels were busy around them. I saw a writing, and copies of it scattered in different parts of the land, giving orders, that unless the saints should yield their peculiar faith, give up the Sabbath, and observe the first day, they were at liberty, after such a time, to put them to death. But in this time the saints were calm and composed, trusting in God, and leaning upon his promise, that a way of escape would be made for them. In some places, before the time for the writing to be executed, the wicked rushed upon the saints to slay them; but angels in the form of men of war fought for them. Satan wished to have the privilege of destroying the saints of the Most High; but Jesus bade his angels watch over them, for God would be honored by making a covenant with those who had kept his law in the sight of the heathen round about them; and Jesus would be honored by translating the faithful, waiting ones, who had so long expected him, without their seeing death.

Soon I saw the saints suffering great mental anguish. They seemed to be surrounded with the wicked inhabitants of earth. Every appearance was against them. Some began to fear that God had left them at last to perish by the hand of the wicked. But if their eyes could have been opened, they would have seen themselves surrounded by angels of God. Next came the multitude of the angry wicked, and next a mass of evil angels, hurrying on the wicked to slay the saints. But as they would attempt to approach them, they would first have to pass this company of mighty, holy angels, which was impossible. The angels of God were causing them to recede, and also causing the evil angels who were pressing around them, to fall back. It was an hour of terrible, fearful agony to the saints. They cried day and night unto God for deliverance. To outward appearance there was no possibility of their escape. The wicked had already commenced their triumphing, and were crying out, Why doesn't your God deliver you out of our hands? Why don't you go up, and save your lives? The saints heeded them not. They were wrestling with God like Jacob. The angels longed to deliver them; but they must wait a little longer, and drink of the cup, and be baptized with the baptism. The angels, faithful to their trust, kept their watch. The time had about come when God was to manifest his mighty power, and gloriously deliver them. God would not suffer his name to be reproached among the heathen. For his name's glory he would deliver every one of those who had patiently waited for him, and whose names were written in the book.

I was pointed back to faithful Noah. The rain descended, the floods came. Noah and his family had entered the ark, and God shut them in. Noah had faithfully warned the inhabitants of the old world, while they had mocked and derided him. And as the waters descended upon the earth, and as one after another were being drowned, they beheld that ark that they had made so much sport of, riding safely upon the waters, preserving the faithful Noah and his family. So I saw that the people of God, who had warned the world of his coming wrath, would be delivered. They had faithfully warned the inhabitants of the earth, and God would not suffer the wicked to destroy those who were expecting translation, and who would not bow to the decree of the beast, or receive his mark. I saw that if the wicked were permitted to slay the saints, Satan and all his evil host, and all who hate God, would be gratified. And O, what a time of triumph it would be for his Satanic majesty, to have power, in the last closing struggle, over those who had so long waited to behold Him whom they loved. Those who have mocked at the idea of the saints going up, will witness the care of God for his people, and their glorious deliverance.

As the saints left the cities and villages, they were pursued by the wicked. They raised their swords to kill the saints, but they broke, and fell as powerless as a straw. Angels of God shielded the saints. As they cried day and night for deliverance, their cry came up before God.

See Genesis chap. 6 & 7, 32:24-28; Psalms chap. 91; Matthew 20:23; Revelation 13:11-17

CHAPTER 37

Deliverance of the Saints

It was at midnight that God chose to deliver his people. As the wicked were mocking around them, suddenly the sun appeared, shining in his strength, and the moon stood still. The wicked beheld the scene with amazement. Signs and wonders followed in quick succession. Everything seemed turned out of its natural course. The saints beheld the tokens of their deliverance with solemn joy.

The streams ceased to flow. Dark, heavy clouds came up, and clashed against each other. But there was one clear place of settled glory, from whence came the voice of God, like many waters, which shook the heavens and the earth. There was a mighty earthquake. The graves were shaken open, and those who had died in faith under the third angel's message, keeping the Sabbath, came forth from their dusty beds, glorified, to hear the covenant of peace that God was to make with those who had kept his law.

The sky opened and shut, and was in commotion. The mountains shook like a reed in the wind, and cast out ragged rocks all around. The sea boiled like a pot, and cast out stones upon the land. And as God spake the day and hour of Jesus' coming, and delivered the everlasting covenant to his people, he spake one sentence, and then paused, while the words were rolling through the earth. The Israel of God stood with their eyes fixed upwards, listening to the words as they came from the mouth of Jehovah, and rolled through the earth like peals of loudest thunder. It was awfully solemn. At the end of every sentence the saints shouted, Glory! Hallelujah! Their countenances were lighted up with the glory of God; and they shone with the glory as did Moses' face when he came down from Sinai. The wicked could not look on them for the glory. And when the never-ending blessing was pronounced on those who had honored God, in keeping his Sabbath holy, there was a mighty shout of victory over the beast, and over his image.

Then commenced the jubilee, when the land should rest. I saw the pious slave rise in triumph and victory, and shake off the chains that bound him, while his wicked master was in confusion, and knew not what to do; for the wicked could not understand the words of the voice of God. Soon appeared the great white cloud. On it sat the Son of man.

This cloud when it first appeared in the distance, looked very small. The angel said that it was the sign of the Son of man. And as the cloud approached nearer to the earth, we could behold the excellent glory and majesty of Jesus as he rode forth to conquer. A holy retinue of angels, with their bright, glittering crowns upon their heads, escorted him on his way. No language can describe the glory of the scene. The living cloud of majesty, and unsurpassed glory, came still nearer, and we could clearly behold the lovely person of Jesus. He did not wear a crown of thorns; but a crown of glory decked his holy brow. Upon his vesture and thigh was a name written, **KING OF KINGS AND LORD OF LORDS**. His eyes were as a flame of fire, his feet had the appearance of fine brass, and his voice sounded like many musical instruments. His countenance was as bright as the noon-day sun. The earth trembled before him, and the heavens departed as a scroll when it is rolled together, and every mountain and island were moved out of their places. And the kings of the earth, and the great men, and the rich men, and the chief captains, and the mighty men, and every bondman, and every freeman, hid themselves in the dens and in the rocks of the mountains. And said to the mountains and rocks, Fall on us, and hide us from the face of him that sitteth on the throne, and from the wrath of the Lamb: for the great day of his wrath is come; and who shall be able to stand?

Those who a little before would have destroyed God's faithful children from the earth, had to witness the glory of God which rested upon them. They had seen them glorified. And amid all the terrible scenes they had heard the voices of the saints in joyful strains, saying, Lo, this is our God, we have waited for him, and he will save us. The earth mightily shook as the voice of the Son of God called forth the sleeping saints. They responded to the call, and came forth clothed with glorious immortality, crying, Victory! victory! over death and the grave. O death, where is thy sting? O grave, where is thy victory? Then the living saints, and the resurrected ones, raised their voices in a long, transporting shout of victory. Those sickly bodies that had gone down into the grave came up in immortal health and vigor. The living saints were changed in a moment, in the twinkling of an eye, and caught up with the resurrected ones, and together they meet their Lord in the air. O what a glorious meeting. Friends whom death had separated, were united, never more to part.

On either side of the cloudy chariot were wings, and beneath it were living wheels; and as the cloudy chariot rolled upward, the wheels cried, Holy, and the wings, as they moved, cried, Holy, and the retinue of holy angels around the cloud cried, Holy, Holy, Holy, Lord God Almighty. And the saints in the cloud cried, Glory, Alleluia. And the chariot rolled upward to the holy city. Before entering the holy city, the saints were arranged in a perfect square, with Jesus in the midst. He was head and shoulders high above the saints, and head and shoulders above the angels. His majestic form, and lovely countenance, could be seen by all in the square.

See 2 Kings 2:11; Isaiah 25:9; 1 Corinthians 15:51-55; 1 Thessalonians 4:13-17; Revelation 1:13-16, 6:14-17, 19:16

CHAPTER 38

The Saints' Reward

Then I saw a very great number of angels bring from the city glorious crowns; a crown for every saint with his name written thereon; and as Jesus called for the crowns, angels presented them to him, and the lovely Jesus, with his own right hand, placed the crowns on the heads of the saints. In the same manner, the angels brought the harps, and Jesus presented them also to the saints. The commanding angels first struck the note, and then every voice was raised in grateful, happy praise, and every hand skillfully swept over the strings of the harp, sending forth melodious music in rich and perfect strains. Then I saw Jesus lead the redeemed company to the gate of the city. He laid hold of the gate and swung it back on its glittering hinges, and bade the nations who had kept the truth to enter in. There was everything in the city to feast the eye. Rich glory they beheld everywhere. Then Jesus looked upon his redeemed saints; their countenances were radiant with glory; and as he fixed his loving eyes upon them, he said, with his rich, musical voice, I behold the travail of my soul, and am satisfied. This rich glory is yours to enjoy eternally. Your sorrows are ended. There shall be no more death, neither sorrow, nor crying, neither shall there be any more pain. I saw the redeemed host bow and cast their glittering crowns at the feet of Jesus, and then, as his lovely hand raised them up, they touched their golden harps, and filled all heaven with their music, and songs to the Lamb.

I then saw Jesus leading the redeemed host to the tree of life, and again we heard his lovely voice, richer than any music that ever fell on mortal ear, saying, The leaves of this tree are for the healing of the nations. Eat ye all of it. Upon the tree of life was most beautiful fruit, which the saints could partake of freely. There was a most glorious throne in the City, and from under the throne proceeded a pure river of water of life, as clear as crystal. On either side of this river of life was the tree of life. On the banks of the river were beautiful trees bearing fruit which was good for food. Language is altogether too feeble to attempt a description of heaven. As the scene rises before me I am lost in amazement; and carried away with the surpassing splendor and the excellent glory, I lay down the pen, and exclaim, O what love! What wondrous love! The most exalted language cannot describe the glory of heaven, nor the matchless depths of a Saviour's love.

See Isaiah 53:11; Revelation 21:4, 22:1-2

CHAPTER 39

The Earth Desolated

I then beheld the earth. The wicked were dead, and their bodies were lying upon the face of the earth. The inhabitants of earth had suffered the wrath of God in the seven last plagues. They had gnawed their tongues for pain and had cursed God. The false shepherds were signal objects of Jehovah's wrath. Their eyes had consumed away in their holes, and their tongues in their mouths, while they stood upon their feet. After the saints were delivered by the voice of God, the rage of the wicked multitude was turned upon each other. The earth seemed to be deluged with blood, and dead bodies were from one end of the earth to the other.

The earth was in a most desolate condition. Cities and villages, shaken down by the earthquake, lay in heaps. Mountains were moved out of their places, leaving large caverns. The sea had thrown out ragged rocks upon the earth, and rocks had been torn out of the earth, and were scattered all over its surface. The earth looked like a desolate wilderness. Large trees were rooted up, and were strewn over the land. Here is Satan's home, with his evil angels, through the 1000 years. Here they will be confined, and wander up and down over the broken surface of the earth, and see the effects of his rebellion against God's law. The effects of the curse which he has caused, he can enjoy through the 1000 years. Limited alone to the earth, he will have no privilege of ranging around to other planets, to tempt and annoy those who have not fallen. Satan suffers in this time extremely. Since his fall his evil traits have been in constant exercise. He is then deprived of his power, and left to reflect upon the part he has acted since his fall, and to look forward with trembling and terror to the dreadful future, when he must suffer for all the evil he has done, and be punished for all the sins he has caused to be committed.

Then I heard shouts of triumph from the angels, and from the redeemed saints, which sounded like ten thousand musical instruments, because they were to be no more annoyed and tempted by the Devil, and the inhabitants of other worlds were delivered from his presence and his temptations.

Then I saw thrones, and Jesus and the redeemed saints sat upon them; and the saints reigned as kings and priests unto God, and the wicked dead were judged, and their acts were compared with the statute book, the word of God, and they were judged according to the deeds done in the body. Jesus, in union with the saints, meted out to the wicked the portion they must suffer, according to their works; and it was written in the book of death, and set off against their names. Satan and his angels were also judged by Jesus and the saints. Satan's punishment was to be far greater than that of those whom he had deceived. It so far exceeded their punishment that it could not be compared with theirs. After all those whom he had deceived had perished, Satan was to still live and suffer on much longer.

After the judgment of the wicked dead was finished, at the end of the one thousand years, Jesus left the City, and a train of the angelic host followed him. The saints also went with him. Jesus descended upon a great and mighty mountain, which, as soon as his feet touched it, parted asunder, and became a mighty plain. Then we looked up and saw the great and beautiful City, with twelve foundations, twelve gates, three on each side, and an angel at each gate. We cried out, The City! The great City! It is coming down from God out of heaven! And it came down in all its splendor, and dazzling glory, and settled in the mighty plain which Jesus had prepared for it.

See Zechariah 14:4-12; Revelation 20:2-6, 20:12, 21:10-27

CHAPTER 40

The Second Resurrection

Then Jesus and all the holy retinue of angels, and all the redeemed saints, left the City. The holy angels surrounded Jesus, and escorted him on his way, and the train of redeemed saints followed. Then Jesus in terrible, fearful majesty called forth the wicked dead; and as they came up with the same feeble, sickly bodies that went into the grave, what a spectacle! what a scene! At the first resurrection all came forth in immortal bloom; but at the second, the marks of the curse are visible on all. Kings and the noble men of earth come forth with the mean and the low, learned and unlearned together. All behold the Son of man; and those very men who despised and mocked Jesus, and smote him with the reed, and that put the crown of thorns upon his sacred brow, behold him in all his kingly majesty. Those who spit upon him in the hour of his trial, now turn from his piercing gaze, and from the glory of his countenance. Those who drove the nails through his hands and his feet, now look upon the marks of his crucifixion. Those who thrust the spear into his side, behold the marks of their cruelty on his body. And they know that he is the very One whom they crucified, and derided in his expiring agony. And then there arises one long protracted wail of agony, as they flee to hide from the presence of the King of kings and Lord of lords.

All are seeking to hide in the rocks, and shield themselves from the terrible glory of him whom they once despised. As all are overwhelmed and pained with his majesty and his exceeding glory, they with one accord raise their voices, and with terrible distinctness exclaim, Blessed is he who cometh in the name of the Lord.

Then Jesus and the holy angels, accompanied by all the saints, again go to the City, and the bitter lamentations and wailings of the doomed wicked fill the air. Then I saw that Satan again commenced his work. He passed around among his subjects, and made the feeble and weak strong, and then he told them that he and his angels were powerful. He then pointed to the countless millions who had been raised. There were mighty warriors and kings who were well skilled in battle, and who had conquered kingdoms. And there were mighty giants, and men who were valiant, and had never lost a battle. There was the proud, ambitious Napoleon whose approach had caused kingdoms to tremble. There stood men of very high stature, and of dignified, lofty bearing, who had fallen in battle. They fell while thirsting to conquer. As they come forth from their graves, they resume the current of their thoughts where it ceased in death. They possess the same spirit to conquer which ruled when they fell. Satan consults with his angels, and then with those kings and conquerors and mighty men. Then he looks over the vast army and tells them that the company in the City is small and feeble, and that they can go up and take that City, and cast out its inhabitants, and possess its riches and glory themselves.

Satan succeeds in deceiving them, and all immediately commence to fit themselves for battle. They construct weapons of war; for there are many skillful men in that vast army. And then with Satan at their head, the multitude move on. Kings and warriors follow close after Satan, and the multitude follow after in companies. Every company has a leader, and order is observed as they march over the broken surface of the earth to the holy City. Jesus closes the gates of the City, and this vast army surround it and place themselves in battle array. They have prepared all kinds of implements of war, expecting to have a fierce conflict. They arrange themselves around the City. Jesus and all the angelic host with the glittering crowns upon their heads, and all the saints with their bright crowns, ascend to the top of the wall of the City. Jesus speaks with majesty and says, Behold, ye sinners, the reward of the just! And behold ye my redeemed, the reward of the wicked! The vast multitude behold the glorious company on the walls of the City. And as they witness the splendor of their glittering crowns, and see their faces radiant with glory, expressing the image of Jesus, and then behold the unsurpassed glory and majesty of the King of kings, and Lord of lords, their courage fails. The sense of the treasure and the glory which they have lost, rushes upon them, and they have a realizing sense that the wages of sin is death. They see the holy, happy company whom they have despised, clothed with glory, honor, immortality and eternal life, while they are outside of the City with every mean and abominable thing.

See Matthew 23:29; Revelation 6:15-16, 20:7-9, 22:12-15

CHAPTER 41

The Second Death

Satan rushes into the midst, and tries to stir up the multitude to action. But fire from God out of heaven is rained upon them, and the great men, and the mighty men, and the noble, and poor and miserable men, are all consumed together. I saw that some were quickly destroyed, while others suffered longer. They were punished according to the deeds done in the body. Some were many days consuming, and just as long as there was a portion of them unconsumed, all the sense of suffering was there. Said the angel, The worm of life shall not die; their fire shall not be quenched as long as there is the least particle for it to prey upon.

But Satan and his angels suffered long. Satan not only bore the weight and punishment of his sins, but the sins of all the redeemed host had been placed upon him; and he must also suffer for the ruin of the souls which he had caused. Then I saw that Satan, and all the wicked host, were consumed, and the justice of God was satisfied; and all the angelic host, and all the redeemed saints, with a loud voice said, Amen!

Said the angel, Satan is the root, his children are the branches. They are now consumed root and branch. They have died an everlasting death. They will never have a resurrection, and God will have a clean universe. I then looked, and saw the fire which had consumed the wicked, burning up the rubbish and purifying the earth. Again I looked and saw the earth purified. There was not a single sign of the curse. The broken up, and uneven surface of the earth now looked like a level, extensive plain. God's entire universe was clean, and the great controversy was forever ended. Everywhere we looked, everything the eye rested upon, was beautiful and holy. And all the redeemed host, old and young, great and small, cast their glittering crowns at the feet of their Redeemer, and prostrated themselves in adoration before him, and worshiped him that liveth forever and ever. The beautiful New Earth, with all its glory, was the eternal inheritance of the saints. The kingdom, and dominion, and greatness of the kingdom under the whole heaven, was then given to the saints of the Most High who were to possess it forever, even forever and ever.

See Isaiah 66:24; Daniel 7:26-27; Revelation 20:9-15, 21:1, 22:3

Made in the USA
Lexington, KY
13 February 2012